STRONG WOMEN OF THE WEST
(ANTHOLOGY)

CHARLIE STEEL
Tale-Weaver Extraordinaire

STRONG WOMEN OF THE WEST
(ANTHOLOGY)

CHARLIE STEEL
Tale-Weaver Extraordinaire

CONDOR PUBLISHING, INC.
Lincoln, Michigan

STRONG WOMEN OF THE WEST
(Anthology)

by Charlie Steel

March 2021

*Cover and Illustrations by Vladimir Shvachko

(All illustrations property of Condor Publishing, Inc.)

Library of Congress Control Number: 2021933033

ISBN-13: 978-1-931079-30-3

Condor Publishing, Inc.
PO Box 39
123 S. Barlow Road
Lincoln, MI 48742
www.condorpublishinginc.com

Printed in the United States of America

DEDICATION

**To all strong women everywhere
and especially to my publisher, Gail Heath, and
my mother, Frances.**

TABLE OF CONTENTS

FLASH OF LIGHT

I saw it for a moment, a white flash, and it was gone. It came from a quarter mile up on the rocky ridge. I immediately turned behind a boulder larger than my buckskin horse and dismounted. There was shade here, and I took time to remove my sombrero. I wiped sweat from my brow on the sleeve of my forearm, grabbed my canteen, and took a drink of lukewarm water. I stood there in the shade of the giant rock and waited.

There was a patch of dried grass. I pulled the bit from my horse's mouth, bent down, and gathered up clumps of long yellow stems. Bucky ate greedily; his teeth made loud chomping sounds in the quiet dry air. I took my sombrero and the canteen and poured a small amount into it, while my four-legged friend sucked at the water and whickered.

"That's it, Bucky. We'll stay here and relax and let that feller on the ridge sweat it out."

I finally tired. Despite the shade, it was quite hot. It was the middle of the day, the sun was high up, and I could only imagine the force of the heat and its effects on that rocky ledge. With my chapeau off my head, I could lean towards the edge of the giant boulder and observe the ridge. I saw another flash, and I knew that the bushwhacker was still there and waiting.

Well, I thought. *Let him wait. Serve him right to sweat and suffer. What does he want me for? I don't know anyone in southern Colorado. I'm just a lone rider, exploring the country. Who is this coyote anyway?*

"Bucky," I whispered. "We'll just spend the afternoon here, and if that hombre don't leave, we'll skedaddle when it gets dark. That suit you, hoss?"

Bucky bent his long neck down and tenderly fastened strong yellow teeth on blades of grass. He pulled with enough force to tear the thin strands away and then chomped loudly.

"My pal Bucky, nothing bothers you. Give a little shade, a little water and grass, and you'll be content to spend the whole day here. If that feller up and shot me, you wouldn't move an inch, would you, boy?"

Bucky bent his head down, found more grass, and raised back to chew. He was a horse without a worry in the world.

"Good old Bucky, best hoss I ever owned," I whispered to him.

In late afternoon I got a mad up and decided to go exploring. First thing I took was a spyglass from my saddlebags and then my Winchester from the scabbard.

"Stay here, Bucky," I said.

For good measure, I tied the horse's reins to a protruding granite rock. Then using the big boulder for cover, I bent low and headed south away from the ridge. Sliding down into a deep ravine, I followed the arroyo and kept to low ground. It was a simple thing to stay out of sight. I walked a long distance before turning towards the ridge.

I came to a rise and went to all fours. I lay down behind a rock and took out my spyglass. It was an old brass affair I had ever since the Great Conflict, and I had used it a lot—both for hunting game and the two-legged kind. I looked through the lens, adjusted it, and saw a man sitting behind a clump of boulders. The gunman had bright yellow hair, all curly like, and he held a rifle. The figure was clothed in buckskins, and when I got a glimpse of a raised head, I had the impression this was a right smart-lookin' feller.

Now, what does a man like that want with me? I wondered.

After another fifteen minutes, I came up the side of the ridge and cocked the hammer on that Winchester. The feller heard me and turned sharply with rifle in hand.

"Now stop there, Mister!" I shouted.

The fool raised his rifle, and I shot. The bullet went high up on the shoulder, right where I aimed. The shooter dropped his gun and grabbed at his wound. I ran uphill, kicked the weapon away, and stood there covering the buckskinned fellow.

"Now why," I asked, "would you want to go and bushwhack a stranger?"

"Wasn't laying for you," responded a feminine voice. "I was up here standing guard for Grandpa Lee."

"You're a woman!" I gasped.

"Yeah!" declared the girl through clenched teeth. "What of it?"

"As a regular habit, I don't shoot women or children.

Now hold still and let me look at that shoulder of yers."

"You shoot me and now I'm supposed to let you fix me up?"

"If you would have put that rifle down, I wouldn't have. You're bleeding, let me help you."

The girl stopped struggling. I took my knife and cut at the stitching on the leather shirt. It exposed a white, smooth-skinned shoulder, with a bullet hole that went deep. It cut above the left collar bone, grazed it, and made a hole clear through the top muscle. It wasn't a bad wound, but it must hurt something fierce.

The young woman leaned her head against a rock. I took off my vest, bunched it up, and made a pillow for her. I stood up and whistled loudly. On the third note, Bucky pulled his reins free and came out from behind the rock. I whistled again, and he spotted me. He made a high-pitched whinny in answer.

"Come on, boy!" I shouted.

That critter came trotting forward, reins dangling. Bucky worked his way around boulders and tall rocks and, in a few minutes, climbed up the ridge and came to my hand.

"Good old hoss," I murmured.

As a reward, I poured some water in my hat and let him drink. Then I stooped and handed the girl my canteen. She drank thirstily. Going to my saddlebags, I pulled out a needle and thread. I held the needle under a lit match. I let it cool and threaded it.

"This is going to hurt," I said. "It's a clean wound, but there are a couple holes I got to sew up."

“If you’re going to do that,” said the girl, “at least tell me your name.”

“My friends call me Jake. I’m hoping you’ll be one of them.”

“Not likely,” responded the girl.

“You gonna tell me yours?”

“Grandpa calls me Curly.”

“Well, Curly, glad to know you.”

I took a shirt from my saddlebags to use for bandages. With my knife, I cut it into strips. The wounds were oozing blood. I mopped it up as best I could.

“Here, hold this cloth,” I said.

“Don’t do me any favors,” grimaced the girl. “You just treat me like any other man.”

“Nawww, can’t do it. You’re a right purty gal, and you’ll have to face up to it. Now, while I’m doing this, suppose you explain who you were waiting to bushwhack.”

“Grandpa Lee,” gasped the girl at the first bite of the needle.

“Go on,” I said, pushing hard and pulling on the thread. “Keep talking.”

“Grandpa Lee, he’s sick. He sent me up here to watch the trail. Grandpa owns this land. Rustlers have been taking our stock. It’s a man named Caldweller. We figure he and his men are trying to steal the place.”

“I see,” I said, working quickly to sew up the first bullet hole.

My fingers were greasy with blood. When I finished, I tied the thread in a looping knot and wiped my hands on my bandanna. I needed more thread, so I went and got it.

Then I commenced working on the back shoulder. I should have cauterized both with a hot knife, but I was reluctant to leave a brand on the girl. I tied up the wounds as best I could, but the back still oozed.

"Don't move," I said. "You lie down and stay still. If it doesn't stop bleeding, I'll have to cauterize it."

"Do what you have to," said the girl through tight jaws.

I watched her. Her face was flushed. Beads of sweat showed on her pretty forehead. She was brave, all right. That clipped collar bone and torn shoulder muscle must hurt something awful. The girl settled back, but she was far from relaxed. I stared at her. She had her eyes closed and didn't see me doing it. She filled out those buckskins in a way no man ever could. Her short curly hair cropped close around her lovely head was something new. On her, it looked good. Blue eyes flashed open, and I was caught.

"What you looking at, Mister?" she shouted angrily.

"You!" I said. "You're about the best looking filly in buckskins I've seen in a crow's age."

"Oh yeah!" she drawled. "Well, don't let it give you ideas!"

"Calm down," I said. "I ain't gonna harm you."

"Sure! You've already done that!"

She hurt my feelings, but I ignored her while I bent down and looked at her wounds. Blood soaked her buckskin shirt, but the bleeding had stopped.

"You're in luck," I said. "Just lie back, and take it easy. If you start that shoulder to bleeding again, it won't be good."

"I can't stay here," whispered the girl. "I got to look

after Grandpa Lee. And I got to watch this pass."

The girl tried to sit up and went into a sort of faint. I let her close her eyes and sleep.

"Best thing for her," I muttered.

I took my bandanna, poured water over it, and placed it against her forehead. Sitting there, I stared at her. I wondered why she and her grandpa come to live way out here.

Bucky stepped forward and gave me a shove with his head. I stood up and stroked the neglected fellow between his ears.

"She's really something," I whispered. "Ain't she? Wonder how old she is. You think once she gets over the shooting, she'll like me?"

Bucky nickered and then shook his head.

"Gee, hoss," I said. "Thanks a lot."

* * *

That night and through the next two days, the girl had a raging fever. I did everything I could to try to stop it. In one of her lucid moments, I asked her where water was, and she pointed. I walked down the ravine, around a hill, and found her horse next to a spring and pond. I went back and carried the girl down. Without opening her wound, I carefully laid her in the cool water until her fever broke. I remembered her talking about her sick grandfather, but there was nothing I could do about that.

* * *

That night, the girl lay on her bedroll. Her shoulder hurt

and every time she moved the wrong way, she woke up.

I should hate him, thought Curly. *But he is right smart-looking. And he did fix me up good. Maybe I shouldn't have pointed my rifle at him. Not the first time I did some darn dumb thing. How long has it been since I met a decent man? I bet Jake is short for Jacob."*

* * *

The morning of the third day, Curly had just finished eating a can of beans when I heard horses coming. I faded back behind some boulders, my Winchester in hand. Five riders came to the spring as if they owned it.

"Well," said a big-bellied rider. "Looks like there was trouble, little lady."

"I'm no lady, Caldweller!" replied the girl.

"Appears you were shot!" said the intruder.

"Yeah!" said the girl. "What of it?"

"What happened?"

"None of your business!" she replied. "If you need to know, I shot the hombre."

"You did?" responded Caldweller.

"Yeah," said the girl, and then she drew a little pistol from someplace in her clothing. She aimed it at the rancher and cocked it.

"Now wait a minute, Alice," said Caldweller. "No need to get riled!"

"I told you to never call me that! I'm Curly, and that's my name. Use it!"

"Okay, Curly. Whatever you say. You know we came to make another offer to Lee."

“He ain’t selling, nor am I! You’ve been told. Now git off this ranch!”

I saw the other riders place hands on pistol butts. One was making a draw. I shot the gun out of his hand. Remaining hidden behind rock, I let them guess where the shot came from.

“Who did that?” asked Caldweller. “Is that you, Lee?”

“Nawww!” I shouted. “I’m one of Lee’s hired hands! Now turn those horses and git!”

“Did your Grandpa go and hire riders?” snarled Caldweller to the girl.

“He did,” she answered. “Now, get off our land. And if you know what’s good for ya, you’ll not come back.”

Caldweller hesitated. I took aim and knocked off the rancher’s hat. Their horses jumped, and two began bucking. The five struggled to maintain their mounts. One rider fell heavily to the ground.

“All right,” I shouted from behind cover. “That’s enough fooling. Get that man on his hoss and ride out of here! Now!”

The horses settled down. The fallen man grabbed reins and mounted. All five turned and headed back down the trail.

“I’ll shoot the next trespasser!” shouted the girl.

When the riders disappeared, I came out from cover. The girl’s face was snow white. The altercation had taken all of her new gained strength.

“You’re some gal, Alice,” I said.

Wide blue eyes flared.

“Why you!”

Then she angrily grasped a small stone in her right hand and threw it with all her strength. The rock struck me square in the chest, and it hurt. I heard her gasp in pain, and I went to her and kneeled down.

"Serves you right, Alice," I said gently.

Instinctively, I came close, then put one hand to her forehead and felt her brow. It was cool to the touch.

"Your fever's gone," I said.

"Not necessarily, Jake," she whispered.

The girl looked up at me and smiled.

"The only time you can call me Alice," she said, "is moments like this."

I sat down beside her. Alice, wincing in pain, stretched her head up and kissed me full on the lips. She surprised me. They were as soft as Bucky's muzzle.

"Say, Alice," I said. "I should have found and shot you *long* before this!"

INTO THE MOUNTAINS

Climbing the narrow game trail, I looked behind. There was nothing but empty space for a drop of two miles. Bright moon and starlight illuminated everything in the open and probed into the recesses of deep dark shadows. Such a sight was too much for my mind to absorb. The vast distance made an unending, beckoning call to my spirit. If I answered, I would let go and fall endlessly into the chasm—flying, drifting, and descending to a certain glorious death. I wrested my concentration from this enchanting and deadly view and continued the steep climb.

Nearly every action in these mountains courted destruction. I could slip and fall, and it would mean the end. Up here, a broken leg was a death sentence. A lone mountain man like me would never be missed and never found, except by coyotes, buzzards, and other critters and vermin. An Indian might happen upon my carcass and surmise a tale of my travels.

Missteps were not the only paths to disaster. Living creatures walked or slithered, or stalked. Wolves, catamounts, bears, packs of coyotes, and rattlesnakes would prey upon anyone who got caught in the wrong place at the wrong time. Utes, Cheyenne, Arapaho, Sioux, and Apache all traveled this country. They would slay a white man for his belt or for the pure hateful pleasure of wiping out any intruder who dared come into their lands. Even a wounded antlered deer could rise up and gore a man. Everything about these mountains meant certain death to anyone who was not careful. And I—well—I am a cautious man when it comes to protecting my hide. That's why I'm traveling at night to avoid the Indians.

About a year back, I was chased up here by a band of Utes. Can't say as I blame them; this is their land. Somehow they managed to track me over solid rock for a far piece before I lost them. I hid along the snowbelt above the timberline in a jumble of boulders, pondering a safe time to come down. Up there, where the snow melted and formed a little stream, I found some color. A blizzard came early, and I left fast. Couldn't chance leaving tracks for those Utes to follow. I waited all winter to go back up and try to find that spot. A little gold could turn into a lot if I was smart and fortunate enough to hit on the mother lode.

Returning this time, I traveled light. It was a hard decision to leave my .45 Hawkins behind. I nearly couldn't do it. Instead, I carried two percussion single-shot pistols in holsters on my belt. I figured that if I had to use a gun up here, I would call in any Indian, mainly Ute, and would be a dead man anyway.

Along with the pistols, I toted a short bow that I was good with and a quiver of arrows. They were for hunting. If I found gold, the dried jerky and corn crammed in the pack on my back would not last me long. Even if I brought down a deer with an arrow, there was the problem of building a fire and cooking. The least flames, reflection, or bit of smoke would bring those Utes running. All I wanted was to make a cold camp, chew on jerky and corn, and stay just long enough to find myself some gold—enough to last me a long time.

I knew it would be a puzzle trying to find that place again. Up here in the mountains, water runoff each season changes the landscape. What was recognizable one year could suddenly transform into a totally different scene the next. Rushing torrents sometimes pushed boulders the size of cabins off ledges. Raging water could strip a bit of land bare of topsoil and expose solid rock. Further down the mountain, flowing rivers could wipe out trails. Truth be told, it could take an entire section of ponderosa pines along with mud and rocks and pile them up every which way.

It was almost dawn when I reached where I thought I had found that little bit of color last year. I was once again near the top, where the snowline remained. Hard as I tried, I could not find the same spot or the little runoff stream that held the gold. Everything was vastly changed. Maybe the gold itself was gouged out by a torrent of snowmelt and swept off and down the mountain. I wondered if I had risked my life for nothing by coming back into Ute land. Deciding to stay and look anyway, I estimated where I was last year and set up a little camp among a jumble of boulders. Even in June, it was cold up here. I took off my pack, unrolled tarp and blanket, and covered up. Good thing I had a heavy elk jacket and buckskins. I would stay as warm as a man could, without a fire. I was at the top of the world, and any kind of reflection could be seen for a long ways.

A man like me, in the shape I was in, didn't need much sleep. I was up at dawn and began digging. There were rivulets of water coming off the snowpack, as I panned for color. Now and then, I would find flakes but nothing substantial. I was sure there was a pocket of gold that eroded down the mountain. If only I could have stayed last year and looked. But now, it was hopeless. Still, I camped several days, searching and not finding anything worthwhile. It was a wild goose chase, and I had missed the golden egg.

Well, I thought. Since I'm here. I might as well sample every little runoff stream on the way back down. Maybe I'll get lucky and find a bit of color. Sure would like to pan enough to make it worth risking my hide.

I knew I wasn't much of a prospector, more a trapper and mountain man than anything else. I had come a long way in divorcing myself from society. As some of my more colorful kind had warned, "Don't have no truck with them flatlanders." So, giving heed to their words, I vowed to live and die alone.

Coming down the mountain was, sure enough, more manageable than going up. It was pure pleasure to descend. More than three quarters along the way, I came to a pretty rushing cold mountain stream and decided to pan. All the time, I kept a sharp watch and didn't take a step without looking hard. As I advanced, I scooped out some gravel and water in my pan and then sort of slid into cover. Now and then, I found a tiny nugget or some flake. These I put in a leather poke. I wouldn't get rich this way, but it was something. Maybe I would get enough to buy me my summer supplies.

I heard something. I stopped and lay low, setting the pan beside me. I worked out my collapsed bow and managed to string it. I nocked an arrow and waited. The sun rose higher, and it was getting warm on my back. The stream before me gurgled, and a cool wind blew. Birds stopped chirping. Once I thought I heard a moan. It sounded almost human, wounded, and in pain. I waited.

An hour went by. Whatever was out there was hurt and alone. I left my pack and pan and began creeping through the brush. From time to time, my buckskins made a whisper on vegetation as I slid forward. I was getting close. Maybe I was a fool to come so deep into these mountains onto Indian land.

Then I saw her. She was lying nearly at my feet, dark eyes gleaming, the clear whites exposed. She lay flat on her back, an iron knife clutched in her right hand. Hatred convulsed her face, and her teeth were revealed in a snow-white grimace. Another step forward and she would have stabbed me, sure. Her buckskin dress blended in with the yellow grass. She was a golden beauty, and no amount of grimacing could hide her good looks.

"Easy," I whispered.

Going to my knees, I put down my bow and backed up a

might. I put both hands up, palms exposed. She knew what I meant but continued to hold the knife, ready to strike. I couldn't recall many Indian words.

"Think!" I told myself and then whispered. "Mamaci! Paa!"

Near as I could figure, she needed water, and that's what I said. I had my canteen on a strap and carefully removed it from around my shoulder. I took the plug out, and she jumped at the sound. Very slowly, I held it out to her. She studied my face, judging me. There were beads of sweat on her forehead, and I watched her lick her lips. I looked down at her legs and saw that her dress was hiked up a bit. The right lower leg was bent slightly below the knee. There was bruising and swelling.

"Paa!" I said again and shook the canteen; some water spilled out.

She licked her lips again. This was getting us nowhere. I put the plug back in, lay the canteen next to her side, and backed away. Her eyes never left mine as she picked up the container. With her teeth, she bit down and pulled out the stopper. Then she quickly put the spout to her lips, upended the thing, and drank deeply. She was very thirsty, and I smiled at the sound of her gulping. Abruptly, she put the canteen down, and it fell on its side. Water gurgled out onto the hard, dry ground. She dropped her eyes for a moment to look and then flashed them back up to watch me again.

"Tog'oiak!" she said.

I was fairly sure that meant thank you.

"You're welcome," I replied.

She didn't seem to understand English, and I sure didn't speak much Ute or any other Indian language.

"Hurt!" I said, pointing at her leg. "I fix."

Again she stared at me. She finally lowered that knife of hers. I backed away and, finding the proper sticks under a large cottonwood, I returned and placed them at her feet. I pointed to her leg. She narrowed her eyes, sighed, and put the knife back in a sheath on her belt.

Cautiously, I eased forward on my knees. She had managed to sit up, and I could see it pained her. I motioned for her to lie down. She did so, hesitantly. Now she was feet first towards me. She wore leather moccasin boots. They were decorated with various beads and designs, as were parts of her dress. Perhaps this young woman was someone of importance. No doubt, at her age, she was married. I was a fool for remaining and helping her. Still, I would not leave her like this. She was in pain, and a wild animal could come along, and…

I hitched up her skirt a bit. She raised her head up to see what I was doing. I didn't blame her. Several times I had seen a broken bone set, but I had never done it. I began to feel around the swelling. There was no sound from her, and I looked at her face. She was lying back, and I could tell it pained her. Here I was on a Ute Mountain, in Ute territory, with a Ute female with a broken leg. What did I think I was doing? I had no idea how to set this break.

I finally got enough gumption to push down hard. I felt and heard bone against bone. There came a slight whimper from the girl. It must have hurt something awful. A broken bone jutted up just below the skin. It looked to me like this was a two-man job—one person to hold and pull on the leg, while another set it. What was I to do? I stood up and paced back and forth, trying to think. The girl watched me. I finally went looking and found a place where two stout saplings grew up and turned into small trees. They were close enough together that I could jam her ankle between them, tie it to the base, and then try to set the leg.

I went back and tried to figure out how I would explain this. I cleared an area, picked up a stick, and began drawing in the dirt. She watched me.

"Do you understand?" I asked her.

Of course, she didn't. I finally went back for my pack and pan and brought them to her. I set the pack beside her. I searched in it and found some leather strings. I showed them to her and then pointed to the pictures. Then I quickly reached down and, sliding my hands under the girl's back and legs, picked her up. She began to protest, but I used all my strength. She didn't weigh much more than a hundred-pound sack of rice. I carried her to the twin cottonwood trees and set her down. She let go of her firm grip on my shoulder.

Bending to one knee, I took hold of the injured leg. Carefully I placed her foot between the two small trees. That must have hurt her something fierce, but she didn't make a sound. Then I tied her ankle firmly so that she could not raise it up. I made her lie flat, her head lower than her feet. Next, I took a thin rope I had in my pack and tried to tie it to one of her wrists. She protested and angrily shook her head. I drew another crude drawing in the dirt. This one showed her arms stretched tightly above her shoulders and tied to a tree. Then I pantomimed me pushing down hard on her leg.

I stopped and watched her face and eyes. I put up my hands to ask. She stared at me a long time and then reluctantly nodded her head. I cut the rope in half, tied each end to her wrists, and pulled her arms back above her head. She tried to watch what I was doing but couldn't. I wrapped the two ropes around a tree trunk and pulled them taut. The girl groaned once. Then I tied the rope off.

As quickly as I could, I returned with the four splints and rope. When I was ready, I set everything I would need close beside me and began to push on her leg. When I thought I had the right combination, I shoved hard. The bone snapped together, and the girl gasped in pain. I rapidly placed the splints and wrapped the rope around them. When I finished, I examined my work. It was a right smart job; she wouldn't be bending that leg any time soon.

I helped her sit up and lean against a boulder. There was sweat on her face; I wiped it away. I put my blanket behind her back and let her rest. She examined my work and looked up at me. For the first time, there was a hint of a smile. I retrieved my canteen, filled it at the river, and brought back fresh cold water for her to drink.

"Tog'oiak!" she said once again, then fell into a deep sleep.

* * *

After several hours, the young woman awoke with a start. She calmed a bit when she saw that I was resting against a rock a fair piece away from her. We didn't communicate very well at first. By gesturing and drawing pictures in the dirt, we managed to get a start. She drew a cave and pointed. I carried her there, splint and all. It was the perfect place with tall brush completely covering the mouth. It was totally hidden from view. I went into its cool darkness, set her down gently on the ground, and then went back for my pack.

The next morning I removed the wrapping. I saw I had made it too tight and cut off some of the circulation. I removed it in time so that I thought there was no damage. She tried to tell me her Indian name, but I could not pronounce it. I began to call her "girl" and realized that was not appropriate.

"Zack!" I told her. "My name is Zack."

She said a name and pointed to herself with her right hand. I tried but could not say it; she held her hand over her mouth and giggled.

"Sally," I said, pointing at her. "Sally."

She thought about that and then smiled.

"Sally!" she said, pointing to herself.

After that, it was obvious that she would learn my language much faster than I was going to learn hers. Smarter, I guess, or maybe English is easier to speak than Ute.

The cave was a godsend, it protected and sheltered us from discovery and dangers of all kinds. As days passed, the splints chafed and rubbed Sally's skin. As long as she remained still, I removed them, and let her lie there in the afternoon sun. Each night, I applied them again. This continued for many weeks. I dare not let her walk on the broken leg, so she lay at the mouth of the cave, saying little.

A month passed. All that time we lived mostly on rabbits. One morning I went to check my snares, and when I returned with a catch, Sally was standing on her good leg and hobbling around on a forked crutch. It was then we heard a noise and a grunting voice. We faded back into the opening. I had been careful not to cut anything growing in front of the cave, and our tracks would be hidden under the brush.

We waited, heard voices and movement. Worried about being trapped inside, I crawled out and hid behind boulders. The cave opening was relatively small. A curve of rock hid most of it. I saw they were Ute warriors, looking for someone—for her, I had no doubt. I thought she would call out. She didn't, and the searchers moved on. It was then I realized she was hiding from her own tribe.

After they were gone, I heard Sally's soft voice whispering beside me.

"Sally, run," she said. "Sally not like smelly man. He who made me, tell me to go live with man. I run and hide!"

"He who made you, your father? He is a Chief?"

"Yes, fa-ther, big Chief!"

So now I understood about her decorated moccasins and dress. Perhaps I was in more trouble than I imagined. I envisioned my body tied over a hot fire, and shuddered.

* * *

When Sally started walking on her own without the crutch, she did fairly well. But there was a slight limp that did not go away. I felt her leg; there was a lump there beneath the muscle. It did not look as straight as it should be. Still, I think she was lucky; it could have not set at all or gone gangrene. I had seen that, too. I wasn't proud of my work but was glad it healed, and she could walk.

"See!" she said, smiling. "Sally walk good!"

I did not tell her that she had a limp, and wondered what would happen if she had to run. I guess, like me, she was happy it healed and that she could use it. It was a very bad break. Perhaps a doctor could have done no better.

We left the cave and made our way down on the rolling grasslands. I led her north, and we followed the Front Range of the Rockies. The snow-capped peaks were visible above us as we traveled through foothills of red cedar and pinion. Here I was, a confirmed bachelor with a golden-skinned, dark-haired, Indian beauty. I couldn't take her back, and I couldn't leave her. We did not talk of the future; she just walked by my side, the two of us traveling and living off the land.

We came to my small cabin on the prairie, and she moved in. I put up a kind of buffalo skin wall to give her some privacy. I had a little money but understood when that ran out, I would no longer be able to buy supplies. I pondered on how I could provide for a woman properly. I worried about her dress and her Indian manner and knew what people would say and how they would react. There was no way I would take her into the little village or to the general store. Yet, she made it plain she was eager, curious about how I lived and about white people.

I worried that she was unhappy every time I left her to

go to town. It was quite a hike to go for provisions, and on those days, I would be gone a long while. Sally didn't say much, but I could tell she was furious that I left her alone. Seems I had to go more often since I had to tote back supplies enough for two. I figured there was a need for some type of animal and conveyance to fetch provisions.

I really didn't have the money but managed to barter for two mustangs by cutting a few cords of wood. When I returned with the mounts, I got the scheme to dress her in pants and get her a sombrero that hid her features. She put on an over-large jacket and tucked her hair up under the hat so that the sombrero hid her face. Then we went to town. She enjoyed every minute of it.

* * *

Sally was smart. She learned to speak English well enough. That first time in town, the young woman looked at everything. I swear she picked up and examined nearly every object in that store. After an hour, the owner got upset. I finally bought some gewgaws to make him and Sally happy. Where she would wear the jewelry or for whom I did not know. Mighty impractical, I thought, but she seemed excited when I spent the last of my money on the rings, chain, and necklace with the red pendant. When we got back to the cabin, she put them on and paraded around, showing them to me.

"Zack good man! Treat Sally fine!"

Then for the first time, she put her arms around my neck and kissed me.

"Zack make good. Be Sally's man!"

Then I knew I was in trouble. I couldn't say no to her. I got a preacher in another town, far from where we lived, to marry us. He wasn't none too pleased to hitch an Indian to a white. My stern voice and my hand on one of my pistols convinced him to continue. Then, when I pulled ma's gold wedding band out of my possibles bag and slid it on Sally's slender finger, that preacher gave me a look that would have drowned a muskrat. On the way back, I tried to explain to Sally what we were in for.

"Sally," I said. "You're Ute, and I'm white. Our two people fight and kill each other."

"I not kill you today, Zack, too soon," she teased, grinning. "We just married."

Sally patted the knife she always wore at her waist. I must have looked surprised, and to be certain, I was. This was not the same quiet little Indian gal I had been lookin' out for. She laughed and waved her hand side to side, watching the sun reflect off the gold wedding band.

"I know how to treat Zach. I will be good strong Ute wife. You not be sorry you marry Sally."

Now, truth be known, a woman was a mystery to me. I had parlayed a time or two with a few fancy doves down at a cantina, but hearing how a man might get in trouble with such gals, I moseyed out when they started warming up. But this young woman I just married—why, she wasn't even the same person I rode in with that morning. She was strong-willed, and I suddenly realized there was much about my new wife I didn't know. Her carefree mood broke, and words no longer rippled with playfulness.

"I speak my mind now," said Sally. "White man tries to take Ute land!"

"Yes, and that's not right, but they won't never stop," I answered.

"Many whites bad, but not Zack."

"Sally, we are two different people come together. You ran from your father and your tribe, and I ran from the whites. You and I fit together, but we do not fit with Utes or the whites."

"Yes. Very sad. My people kill you; your people kill me."

"That's what I'm trying to say."

"Then Zack and Sally live away from both," she said.

"Yes, I guess I can trap and sell furs. It won't be grand, but I can keep you in necessities. I promise."

Again the white teeth gleamed, and the corners of her mouth turned up in a grin.

"No worry. I tell you, I make Zack good wife. You tell me about yellow metal and its worth. I know place where it stays."

"Is it up on the Ute mountains?"

"Yes. The place I know like my hand. We be brave, sneak, and take!" said Sally, smiling.

"Do you think we would live through it?" I asked.

"You say whites need money, you need money. We go plenty quick and get gold. Come home to Zack's cabin, make babies, be happy, live long time."

Guess my face turned kinda sunburnt. But while I was pondering on her words, we approached a little cottonwood thicket next to a small winding creek. Sally pulled reins and slid down from her horse. I didn't say anything, figuring she was looking for a necessary stop.

She stepped to my horse. Reaching up, Sally took my hand and pulled me down from the saddle.

"It's early," I said. "If we keep riding, we can make it home afore dark."

"Zack sometimes smart, but in this, I'm thinking not so," she said mysteriously.

Wrapping her arms around my neck, she pulled my head down and put her face against mine. Her lips crushed hard and then softened and moved away. I didn't want her to stop.

* * *

We stayed there lying under the blankets in that little copse of cottonwoods. Together we watched the reflection of stars sparkle on the water in the meandering stream.

"Zack, I tell you," she whispered in my ear. "Having each other is enough. You will see."

PRAIRIE GIRL

The struggling wagon train stopped and circled for the evening. Tired oxen and mules stood, heads hanging and silent in their traces. Saddled horses were also abused with too much riding, too little food and water, and little rest. The weary pioneers dragged their feet as they tiredly went through the well-practiced motions of unharnessing the animals and setting up camp. This was a dry stop. There was no water, and the last promised stream did not flow. The water barrels were nearly empty, and all the canteens were drunk dry. Weary desperation showed on the animals' dust-covered features and on the cracked and sunburned faces of every man, woman, and child.

Five-year-old Dorthea jumped down from the back of Ma and Pa's wagon. She was sick of all this traveling. It wasn't any fun, and besides, she was thirsty and hungry. It had been a long time since she had eaten or quenched her thirst. Ma, Pa, and her older brother and sister were grumpy and always arguing. Too bad they didn't stay on the farm back in Ohio. Pa was wrong about this country being a land of milk and honey. Dorthea loved honey and a cool refreshing glass of milk. She hadn't had any since leaving Independence, Missouri.

Dorthea thought for once she would go off and explore. Some interesting bushes were growing in a clump off yonder; she ducked behind the wagon and kept going. There was some kind of hill or incline; she scurried up it, the growing scrub and salt bushes hiding her from view. On the other side, the sandy hill descended steeply. The little girl slipped on a stone, lost her footing, and slid down and down. Her dress slipped up behind her and tore as her undergarments made contact with the soil. Her bottom rubbed hard against hot stones and sand, and it hurt. Coming to a sudden stop, her feet hit soft ground. She brushed the dirt away from her sore behind, adjusted her underclothes, and pulled down her dusty dress.

It was darker and cooler here in the deep shade of the arroyo. Dorthea looked up; it was a long, long way to the top. Her pa and ma would be very angry.

How will I get out of here? the girl wondered.

Putting a dry tongue on dry lips, she yearned for a cool drink of water. Up ahead, the girl saw movement. It was the darting behind of a coyote. Dorthea followed, putting one foot in front of the other on the smooth, hard-packed bottom of the deep wash. She ran for a moment, and then her throat became too dry, and she slowed down. Around a sharp turn, the child saw another flash of gray and brown, and this time there were two animals. They ran along the wash; Dorthea followed until they disappeared at a sharp twist in the dry watershed.

There began to be thick sand in the wash. Dorthea's

shoes sank in it, it became difficult to walk. The sand was deposited there by a past flood. Further ahead she came to firmer ground. The deep shade was welcoming, with thick grass growing here and there. It was pleasant, and when Dorthea made another turn in the wash, she walked up to a clear pool of water. There were tracks everywhere here in the sandy bottom, but Dorthea didn't pay any attention. She went to her knees and then to her belly, stuck her face and mouth into the cool liquid, and began to drink. As she swallowed, the water burned down her dry throat. This didn't stop her. She kept drinking, over and over, until her thirst was quenched and her empty belly full.

The little girl stood up, and the water felt good sloshing around in her tummy. Dorthea looked ahead and saw another bend, and there, too, lay glistening water. Green grass grew thick and rich. Some kind of deer came toward her, stopped, and stared at the girl. The animal snorted, stamped a back hoof, turned, and disappeared. This was such a lovely spot.

Here, thought Dorthea, *is enough water for Mommy and Daddy and everybody.*

She looked up. The high bank was impossible to climb. Instead, she sat down in a shady spot and settled comfortably on the cool sand. She laid her head back against the wall and rested. It wasn't long before sleep came. Through the late evening, the little girl lay in deep repose. Awaking once, she tiredly went for another drink of water.

I have to get back to the wagon train, it's getting dark, she thought. *But I am so sleepy.*

Again she went to the soft sandy resting place and fell fast asleep. She slept through the night. It wasn't until early morning Dorthea awoke.

She felt guilty and in a panic. Her Ma and Pa would be very angry at her for running away. Her sister and brother would be looking for her. In fact, the entire wagon train would be searching. Again Dorthea took a drink and then turned and hurried back up the arroyo. When she came to the spot where she slid down, she searched for a way up and found none. The child continued on. Despite the coolness of the deep watershed, she began to sweat and became hot and thirsty. She was very hungry now, and her belly hurt. Part of her torn dress dragged. The little girl bent and ripped a piece off. She folded it and stuck it in a small pocket. Now her mother would really be angry.

The sun was high above before Dorthea found a crack in the widening arroyo. Here it was flatter, and the sides were not so steep. She climbed up and out. Keeping her directions, she simply followed the wash back along its bank. When she came to where the wagon train had camped, there was nothing but an empty space and lots of tracks of people, animal hooves, and wagon wheels.

Dorthea cried out in angry frustration and fear. Then she suddenly and tiredly sat down and wept. The hot tears ran down her dusty face.

"Mama!" called the little girl. "Papa!"

She could not believe they had gone and left her.

In sudden panic, the child rose to her feet and ran, following the wagon tracks. She did this for as long as she could, alternating between a run and a quick walk.

Slowly Dorthea continued on for more than an hour before exhaustion overtook her. She sat down in the middle of the trail and stared far ahead. All she saw were tracks disappearing into the distant horizon. In every direction, the prairie looked the same. There was the pastel green of scattered plants, the beige of hard adobe sand, and the yellow of parched grass. This went on for endless miles.

The child buried her face in her hands and wept. Frightened and exhausted, she looked up. A group of men in buckskins stood not more than ten feet away from her—as many as the fingers on her hands. These strange men stared down from brown faces, with dark piercing eyes, and some wore leather bands and feathers in their long black hair.

She knew what they were. Ma and Pa had warned her. If she wasn't good, the Indians would get her.

Well, she thought. *I have been bad, and now the Indians are here.*

If that was how it was to be, she might as well face it, just like her Ma and Pa had taught her. The young girl raised her head in stubborn defiance. She came to her feet, clenched her little fists, and stared back at the Indians.

"My name," she said with a crying gasp, trying to hold back her tears, "is Dorthea."

SAND LILY OF THE DESERT

When the gunshots sounded, the three-year-old child awoke and looked up and out of a crack in the back of the wagon. The explosions continued, as her mother and father arose from the bedding. Father put on his pants and took up a rifle.

"Take the child and hide under the wagon," he ordered.

The father swept the canvas back. Early dawn light flooded into the wagon, and the little girl watched her Pa climb down. Her mother hurriedly grabbed and put on a dress. Still in a nightgown, the child was picked up and carried outside. Inside the circle of wagons, men fought and died. Indians rushed everywhere. There was hand-to-hand fighting; the painted warriors outnumbered the pioneers, and they were winning. Screams, gunshots, arrows, spears, and knives flashed and echoed in the narrow opening. Men, women, and children fell and died.

In desperation, the mother grabbed her daughter, jumped over a wagon tongue, and raced outside into the brush. She carried her little child close to her chest as she ran. At first, it appeared as if she wasn't noticed. Then an arrow flashed, a thump, and a deep shuddering of pain overtook the woman. She ran as far as she could through the tangle of brush and weeds along a narrow dry river bed. The harsh breathing disturbed the child, then her mother dropped her and fell to the ground.

"Listen to me," begged the woman, her breath coming in great gasps. "Go hide now!"

"Is this a game, Mommy?"

"Yes, go hide."

"Will you find me?"

"Go now, sweet pea. Go and find a good place."

"Yes, mommy," the little girl replied.

Looking back repeatedly, the child followed a little game trail along the gully. The noise of the battle decreased with distance. The girl, knowing that something was dreadfully wrong, did as her mommy told her. She spied to her right, above the deep river bed, a rabbit trail leading into a shelter of thick grass and piled wood. Getting on her hands and knees, she crawled along the path. She continued until the jumble of sticks and grass surrounded her. It was cooler inside the shelter, and the sun barely penetrated. The child sat down on the gravel and sand. The noise of the fight in the distance lessened and stopped. The girl waited a long time, but no one came.

* * *

"Come on, Blanche," complained the old miner to his burro. "We aren't halfway home yet."

The burro stopped and hee-hawed. Stinky Pete, knowing Indians were about, grabbed the bridle and clamped strong fingers over nostrils.

"Now, you hush. You want us looking like pincushions?"

They continued on, and then the old man smelled burnt wood. Peering through the brush, he saw color and movement. Going forward, the prospector saw a blur of brown coyotes, running. Buzzards hopped and reluctantly flapped into flight. The remains of burned wagons and corpses lay before him. The burro stepped back and tried to hee-haw. Stinky Pete grabbed nostrils again.

"These poor folk," whispered the man to the burro. "These poor ignorant greenhorns."

Waiting to see if Indians were about, Blanche and Stinky Pete stood and did not move. Deciding they were no longer there, the old man began to examine the remains. It was evident the attack took place the previous dawn. It was unlikely there were any survivors, but he looked. There were too many bodies to bury, and in any case, the coyotes and buzzards would soon complete their calling.

Everything of value was taken by the Indians; the rest burned. The circle's atmosphere was oppressive. The old man grabbed the burro's lead, and with little encouragement, they escaped up the trail. They traveled some distance and came across the partial remains of another body. Two buzzards flew up in front of them. They stepped around and continued up the path. Ahead, the burro stopped and stared into the brush.

"What is it, girl, Indians?" whispered the old man.

There was a faint rustling sound, and then it stopped. Pete stood there quietly as the burro continued to look at a mound of brush. It was evident something was there. The old man got down on his knees and looked into the opening. He saw movement but was not sure what it was.

"Hello," whispered Pete. "If you're from the wagon train, I'm a friend."

There was silence, and then the old man saw a little hand, then another. A blonde head appeared, and a child crawled out of the opening.

"Well, I'll be," said Stinky Pete, taken totally by surprise. "A little girl."

The blonde-haired creature stood. Blanche came near, sniffed, and backed up.

"Is my mommy here?" asked the child.

The old man stood open-mouthed. Closing it, he took a deep breath and started to speak. For the first time in his life, he could not think of anything to say. By nature, Stinky Pete was a solitary man. He had gotten his name because of his aversion to baths. His best and only friend was Blanche, the burro.

"You smell funny," sniffed the girl.

Again the mouth went open. The old man wasn't completely dense; he remembered the woman's remains on the path and put two and two together. She must have brought the child out here to hide and died with the arrow in her back.

"Did your mommy tell you to hide?" asked Pete.

"Yes. I want my mommy."

"She ain't," started the old man and stopped and thought, "she told me to come and get you. Are you ready to go now?"

"Will mommy be coming?"

"No child, she won't."

"Did those bad men get her?"

"Yes, child, they did."

The girl sat down in the dirt and began to cry. She did not wail or scream; she just sat and sobbed. Big fat tears made streaks down her dusty face. Out of all the life experiences the old man ever had, this was the most unique. He had been a loner early on and had traveled all over the West. He had fought and lived with Indians. He had wintered in the mountains, struggled with illness, starvation, and wounds, but never had encountered a situation like this.

"Tarnation, child, don't you cry!"

"I want my mommy," sobbed the little girl.

"Child, crying will never bring her back."

The girl looked up at the miner with big, round, blue eyes. She stared at the wrinkled and bearded face of the old man and then suddenly lifted up her arms to be picked up. Pete hesitated. Not for thirty years had he touched another human being. The girl continued to stare, and the drying tears glistened on soft, round cheeks. Pete stooped down and, with both hands, picked up the child, holding her straight-armed in front of him. He held her with the same caution as he would hold a rattlesnake. Staring into the child's innocent eyes and face, his isolated nature melted, and he slowly brought her close giving her a reassuring hug. To his surprise, she reached as far as she could with her short arms and hugged him back.

"There, there, little girl. You'll be all right now."

Pete couldn't imagine this was true, but he said it anyway.

"You smell funny," the little girl repeated and giggled.

"Your face tickles."

The old man was surprised at all the emotions that coursed through him. The little girl's warm hug felt good, and her immediate acceptance of him startled and delighted the prospector. He also felt embarrassed at her statement and vowed to take a bath and put on clean clothes as soon as he got back to the cave. Not for years had he cared how he smelled.

Pete put the girl on the back of the burro, in front of the supply pack he purchased in Colorado City. Blanche again made to object, and the old man stopped her.

"What's your name, child?" asked Pete.

"Me, Sweet Pea."

"Well, now, that's nice. Maybe we can improve on that later."

The child nodded off while on the back of the burro, and Pete was grateful. He kept a careful watch on the youngster as he walked beside her. If she lost her seat, he would be there to catch her. She snuggled up nicely against the pack.

They made it through the low land. Pete utilized the cover and followed the trail along the dry river bed for many miles. Then they began to climb and came out on rolling prairie. The open country revealed itself in three directions. Pete was heading west, towards the Front Range of Greenhorn Mountain. The peak loomed before them. Blanche stepped easily up and up, and they disappeared into the dense growth of pinion and cedar trees.

After a long climb, they came to the solid rock base of the mountain. Following southward along the granite wall, they arrived at a crevice that expanded into a small hidden cave. This was where the old man and burro lived. Nearby, out of the rock, a trickle of water seeped onto solid granite, overflowed, and disappeared into the ground.

It's a good thing it's summer, thought Pete. That young'un must be cold. But what'll she wear?

He thought of cutting blankets or a tarp, and then he decided he would retrieve his old skills and make her a buckskin outfit. He had a tanned deer hide, enough to make several dresses. He took the child off the burro and carried her into the cave. The best thing for her was sleep. He started to put her on his smelly bedroll but thought better of it. Disgusted with himself, he picked up two of his cleanest wool blankets from a rock shelf with one hand and, still holding the child with his other, made a bed for her on the floor inside the cave. He gently laid her down on that. Removing the pack from Blanche, he let her roam free. She was a pet and would not go far.

Stinky Pete sat down on his favorite rock and stared. This sure upsets the applecart. What do I know about caring for a child? Her kinfolk are lost for sure. He stood, picked up his dirty bedding, and struggled with his conflicting thoughts. What am I going to do now? What if I bring her to town, and someone takes her and treats her bad. Poor young'un. Didn't she put those little arms around me and hug me? Didn't those innocent eyes look up at me and give me her trust? I couldn't possibly take care of her. It's stupid to even think on it. Reckon I just better see how it goes for a spell.

The old man diverted the water into a granite basin he

had carved from the rock. This was a natural cistern he used for washing clothes. It would work well as a bath, although he had never used it as such. He got lye soap out of a pack, and then clean clothes. His modesty and abhorrence of water made him reflect on what he was about to do. Grimly tensing his jaws, he stripped and bathed for the first time in the crystal cold water. He soaped every part of him, quickly and vigorously, sputtering and holding his breath against the powerful soap. Then he jumped out, flicked water from himself, and dressed in clean clothing. Next, he put his dirty clothes and bedding in the water and soaked them. The little girl awakened and came out to him as he was lathering the clothing.

"You wash Sweet Pea?" she asked.

Once again, the old man's mouth hung open.

"No, child, that is something you are going to have to do for yourself. You wait until I'm finished here. I'll heat some water in a kettle for you, and then you can step in this granite tub and clean yourself up."

"What Sweet Pea wear?" she asked, holding out the dirty gray nightie she was in.

"I'll fix you a little dress. You'll see."

The old man finished scrubbing his bedroll and clothes and hung them up to dry. Next, he let clean water run into the basin. He filled a bucket, poured it into a large black kettle, and started a smokeless fire for the water to heat. Pete found the deer hide in the back of the cave. Outside, he measured the little girl. She watched as he cut and stitched a dress for her to wear.

"Here," he said. "You try this on."

The old man pulled the dress over her nightgown. It was a bit baggy but would serve its purpose.

"Sweet Pea look good?"

The old man smiled.

"Yes, child. The next one I cut, I'll be more careful about size."

His first act after making her clothing was to name her Sand Lily. He thought of Daisy, but that was much too common of a name or flower for this lovely child. The Sand Lily was a difficult flower to spot, and it only grew next to springs and in canyons. Pete felt it was a fitting name.

The days passed quickly, and the old prospector got used to having the girl hanging around. With each day, her presence grew upon him. It wasn't long, and the notion of giving her up to strangers left him entirely.

* * *

In the following eleven years, the pattern of the old man's life changed significantly. Before, he had only himself to think of and lived accordingly. When the child came, all that changed.

Since that first day, he had been working to improve their circumstances. He did for Sand Lily what he would never do for himself. The old man homesteaded a hundred-sixty-acre section and got patent to the land. In her early years, he prospected hard for gold and found a few pockets. He cashed in some and saved the rest for a time of need.

Below the cave, he built a cabin. Pete made sure Sandy always had decent clothing. He bought his "niece" books and took suggestions from a schoolmarm in Pueblo on what to teach the child. She learned her three R's. At night, she always had her head in one of the many books he ordered for her. Many evenings, she read aloud to him about things Pete had never imagined. In everything she did, she brought joy.

Pete's ranch was the only one with a permanent spring that flowed all year round. He bought three more homesteads from neighbors who gave up and sold out. Sandy was every bit a tomboy and could ride as well as any cowboy. She helped with the raising of cattle and horses.

Now with a full section, six-hundred-and-forty acres, the cattle and horses were bringing a profit. Part of it was fenced, and Pete built a bunkhouse. He hired four cowhands to run cattle, some on open range. Pete had surprised himself with his success. It was all because of the girl.

* * *

"Sandy, what you got thar?" asked Pete.

She was always bringing little creatures to care for. Gently, she set an injured bird down on a rock next to their old cave. This one looked like a Western Jay with a broken wing.

"Oh!" said Sandy. "Isn't he just lovely?"

She was always saying such things. Pete looked at the girl fondly. He was very grateful this child had come into his life.

"Un-cle Pete?" questioned the young lady.

The old man groaned. He knew that tone of voice. She

was going to ask him something personal. Or perhaps something about her past, or about going to town, or some durned fool thing he wouldn't have an answer for.

"Billy asked me to go to the dance in Colorado City. Can I go, Pete?"

Now, this was something new. He had been dreading her growing up. His temper rose, and his face reddened. The girl looked at him, and Pete choked back an angered response.

"Is it fittin'?" asked Pete. "You're only sixteen years old."

"I'll be seventeen soon. At least that's what you told me. A lot of girls are married at my age."

"I just hired this Billy. I don't know nothin' about him."

"You never talk to anyone, Uncle Pete. You could know him if you wanted to."

There came no reply, only silence.

"How about if we take the wagon and you and Billy talk on the way to the dance?" she suggested.

Pete tried his best to suppress his anger, but his pulse increased. He loved this girl more than life itself, and he would hate to lose her. The time was coming when she would marry, and then what would he do? He had known loneliness. This girl had taken it away and brought the sunshine. He could never survive being alone again.

"Okay, child," answered Pete reluctantly. "If that's what you want, we'll do it."

"You promise to be nice to Billy?"

"Yes, Sandy."

Pete laughed as the girl rushed to him and hugged

him fiercely. Spontaneously, she bent down and kissed his cheek. His face flushed. He would never tell her how much these tender moments meant to him.

"Don't worry, Uncle Pete," said the girl, sensing his deep concern. "I'll never leave you. Whoever I marry has to stay right on this ranch so you can help raise our children."

"You would do that for this old man, child?"

"Yes, Pete. I thought on it long and hard. Ever since you found me and raised me up, I've been happy. I couldn't leave you and this ranch. You've been the best mother and father a girl could ever have."

Pete's eyes flashed in wonderment. She had never said such a thing before. He was overcome with pride.

The girl picked up the injured Jay she had set down. Sandy held it in one hand while mounting her horse with the other. She rode off through the pines to the cabin. There she would put the bird in a cage and nurse it until it was well. Old Pete watched her ride away, and he smiled.

Who would have ever figured rescuing a child, he thought, c*ould so upend the life of an old prospectin' fool like me.*

LIGHT AND SHADOW

The sky was blue and filled with cumulus clouds, some fleecy white and some gray. The sun brightened, and a cloud would intermittently dim its power and create light and shadow. Hour after hour, the contrast alternately played across the land. A warm breeze blew, shaking tree limbs, grass, and bushes. It was a good day to be alive and enjoy what the earth and the Creator provided.

It was after the lunch hour and late to begin chores, but Ben Hawk had not felt well. After lying in bed until twelve, he finally got up and fixed himself coffee. It was not until then that he felt any motivation. Not that much work had to be done, anyway. Ben stepped out on the porch of his cabin and shaded his eyes against the bright light. A large dark cloud began to block out the sun. Moving off the porch, the growing pallor fitted his mood as he went about his daily chores. At 68 and with failing vigor, the old man had stopped ranching on his section spread. All that was left were two draft horses, a black mustang, a milk cow, and chickens.

The cow was mooing in distress. Getting the bucket, the indifferent rancher milked the complaining animal.

When he finished, the cow kicked the container, and the milk spilled onto the ground.

"I ought to sell you. All you do is complain, and I don't drink that stuff anyway."

Ben forked hay into the corral for the horses, pumped water into their trough, and spread cracked corn on the ground for the hens. Not feeling hungry, and weary of his own thoughts, he was just too depressed to gather eggs for late breakfast. Not caring, he went back to the cabin.

"My father would have beat me for being so darn lazy," mumbled Ben. "He never quit. On his last day, he died cuttin' hay."

The sun came out from under a cloud, and once again, light flooded the land. Ben squinted, looked up, and saw three dark forms circling. Hand to forehead, he studied the drifting objects. They were turkey buzzards.

"See something, do you? Well, it ain't me, not today, at least. And it'll be some time if I have anything to say about it."

Going into the old cabin, Ben poured coffee into a porcelain cup and walked back outside, slamming the screen door. He sat in his favorite chair on the porch, relaxed, and the pain in his back and neck lessoned. Eighty acres sloped down off Silver Mountain. He watched the dirt road below; and someone was on it. Dust rose, and as the object came closer, the old man saw it was a horse and buggy.

"Oh no," complained Ben. "Not again. Won't that woman leave me alone? I ain't got nothin' she wants. Not from a dried-up old fool like me."

Ben watched as the buggy reached the fence entrance. The woman got down, opened it, led horse and conveyance through, and closed the wooden gate behind her. As she struggled to climb back up to her seat, the old man laughed.

"She ain't gettin' any younger, neither."

The horse and buggy and its wheels kicked up a long trail of dust as the older woman's whip slapped hide. She guided the contraption up the two-lane trail, past the corral, and to the front of the cabin.

"Howdy, Ben," she called in an energetic tone.

"Hello, Bess," replied the old man. "Somethin' I can do for ya?"

"Well, don't just sit there, come help a lady down."

"Humpf! I saw you didn't have no trouble when you opened and closed the gate."

"Are you going to show any manners, Ben, or just sit there sucking on that Java?"

"Don't you be insultin' my drink. It's called coffee, woman."

"Well, take a sip and get over here! Help me down like the gentleman I know you are."

"This is the West," replied Ben, painfully rising to his feet, "and I ain't no gentleman, and you're no lady."

"If your Mama could hear you now, you'd get the switch."

Ben laughed.

"Got that right."

Crossing the hard-baked ground, Ben reached up a hand, and the woman took it. She was wearing a wide-brimmed hat, but her long thick white hair flowed under it, and down to her shoulders. The sun shone brilliantly into the woman's face as she looked toward Ben. Except for a few wrinkles, she appeared a right handsome lady. Holding the man's hand, Bess put foot to a step-down and swung her ample hip into the old rancher's face. Her corduroy skirt brushed his cheek. She smelled like lilac toilet water, and despite himself, Ben breathed deeply and smiled.

"You're smellin' mighty good, Bess."

Despite herself, the woman blushed, then she reached in behind her seat and pulled out a white flour sack.

"Brought you some vittles, Ben. Package of that coffee you like so much is in there."

"Did you bring peaches?"

"Would I forget that?"

"Good, let's go inside, and you open that airtight, and we'll have some. Come to think on it, I ain't et nothing a'tall this mornin'."

"Ben! How many times have I said you got to eat right."

"Yeah, I know. I just forgot. 'Sides, I weren't hungry."

Together the two walked across the yard. Bess tried to hand the heavy sack to Ben, but his back was to her, so he didn't notice. She carried it up the steps, across the porch, and inside. She dumped the groceries on the rough kitchen table with a thump and a sigh.

"Ben!" she complained. "Your speech and manners are gettin' worse every time I come to visit."

Turning to see what she was complaining about, Ben's face twisted into a reflexive grin.

"Well, don't just stand there smiling," she said. "You get the dishes and forks, and I'll open this airtight. And while you're at it, you can pour me a cup of coffee, too!"

"Bossy old thing, aren't you?" said Ben.

Bess stopped and studied the man's face.

"I swear, I don't know when you're joking and when you're serious. Here I try to do a good turn, and this is the way you talk to me."

"Sorry, Bess," replied Ben. "You'll have to excuse this old man."

"And I do, Ben," she laughed. "I really do. And the only one calling you old is yourself. Why you have a lot of good years left in you. And truth be known, you are a right good-looking fellow."

"Startin' that again?"

"I never finished. Why, if you and I got together, we could hire help and get this ranch to operating the way it should. And you could come live at my place, or we could fix up this one, and together we could run as many as a hundred head. Why we'd be sitting pretty, and you know it."

"Maybe I don't want to be sittin' pretty. Maybe I like it just fine the way I'm gittin' on."

"You call this getting by? Drinking coffee, not eating breakfast, barely having any chores? Why Ben, it's two o'clock in the afternoon, and you haven't even combed your hair!"

She said this and pulled a lock of hair across his forehead.

"Stop that!" exclaimed Ben, reaching up and mussing his mop. "I like it that way. And besides, you shouldn't be so darn familiar."

Bess laughed.

"You vex me, Ben. You surely do. Now sit down and let me dish out these peaches."

The old rancher did as he was told. It was Bess who had to set the table. She opened and poured the thick syrup and bright orange peaches onto the only plates he owned. Finding a clean cup in a cupboard over the dry sink, she poured hot coffee into her cup and placed it on the table. Then she filled Ben's cup, put it in front of him, and sat down. The rancher picked up a fork, stabbed a peach, and took it to his mouth.

"Ben!" complained Bess.

In contrition, the old man lowered his head, and his self-invited guest prayed.

"Lord, bless this food we are about to partake, bless us both, our ranches, and those we love and care about."

"A-men," mumbled Ben, more in habit, than in reverence.

They ate the peaches in silence. That is, Bess did, while Ben kept smacking his lips and making quick sounds of pleasure with every forkful. The woman watched him as he ate, and smiled. When finished, they drank their coffee and stared beyond each other. It was a lengthy silence. After a while, Bess cleared her throat. Ben didn't respond. She did this several times.

"Alright, you stubborn fool, just sit there and ignore me. Pretend I'm not here!"

"Bess, I sure do appreciate the peaches, vittles, and coffee, but dang it, I didn't invite you over here; you did."

"Well!"

"Bess, we've known each other too long for you to be offended."

"How do you know that? How do you know anything about how I feel? Each time I come here, you just sit there and refuse to talk."

"So…"

"So, nothing! This time I'm going to say everything what's on my mind."

"Do you have to?"

"Well, like it or not, I'm going to! Here you sit, you lonely old coot! My spread right next to yours. Nearly two whole sections! Two miles of good graze, and we both have water. And what do you do? Nothing with your ranch. And meanwhile, I sit next door and make a profit. But you know what? I don't get any pleasure out of it."

His only response was a big sigh.

"Ben, you never married. Why, I don't know. And me, I lost Frank nigh twelve years ago. We've been friends nearly all our lives."

"Bess, I ain't nothin but an old man set in my ways, and I don't have anything to…"

"Wrong! Don't you think I could fatten you up and get you to smiling?

"You're right, I don't eat much, but…"

"You sit on this mountain all alone, depressed, not enough work to keep you busy. You don't push yourself, and you're NOT enjoying life. I can fix that."

"I don't think so," sighed Ben. "I'm too old to change now."

"Why you stubborn fool!" exclaimed Bess.

She jumped up and scraped chair legs loudly against the floor, scurried around the table, and shoved her ample body against the startled man. Bending down, she grabbed Ben's head in both hands and forcefully kissed him on the mouth. He tried to twist away, but Bess set her round butt on the table, scraping a dish off and onto the wooden floor where it bounced and broke with a crash. Still grasping Ben's head, she again kissed him firmly. This went on for some time until the old man responded.

Standing up, the woman shook her head provocatively and thick white hair cascaded around her shoulders. Bess went around Ben's chair, and placing her hands on the man's shoulders, began to massage them. She started out gently and then more firmly. It was a slow deep massage into the muscles of his shoulders and back. This went on a long time before she stopped.

It was getting dark by the time she finished.

"Thanks, Bess," said Ben. "That felt mighty good. I don't remember a time I felt better."

Bess's hair was in disarray, and she shook her head to rearrange it and smiled.

"My pleasure, and that's only a sample."

The woman put her hand on Ben's head and stroked his hair.

"That feels good, Bess, don't stop."

She continued, and then the man reached up and took the woman's hand and squeezed. Holding onto it, he arose from the chair, turned and bent down and kissed her hard on the lips. Then Ben went to the stove, opened the firebox, and stuffed in paper and kindling. He lit and threw in a match.

"I'll heat up the coffee, woman," the man said, smiling broadly.

"I brought cheese, bread, bacon, and beans. If you don't mind, I'll fix supper."

"Bess!" replied the elder rancher, a broader smile upon his face. "I've changed my mind. It would be rather nice having you around."

"Ben!" exclaimed Bess in surprised pleasure.

"Soon as we git hitched," said the old man, "you can stay and fix whatever you want, for as long as you want. It'll be just fine by me."

ALICIA'S COURAGE

"The basket of food is under the tarp, husband," Alicia told her tall, handsome man.

She stood near the wagon, squinting into the piercing rays of the early morning sun. Before her, the prairie opened up into vast distances. She looked towards the cottonwoods along the river and thought she saw movement. Staring, she watched but saw nothing more.

"It's wrong for me to go and leave you here without protection," John answered, a frown etched on his youthful face.

Alicia smiled, and the wrinkles of worry and hard work disappeared.

"I won't leave my vegetable garden or the crops unguarded," the woman stubbornly argued, as she crossed her arms above her large belly. "We worked too long planting and watering to lose it to the birds and deer. You know they jump over the fence the first chance they get."

"I know. I thought the scarecrow and those noisemakers we made would scare them away. We can't keep guarding it day and night."

"We have to, and we will. Besides, you promised to

buy two guard dogs this trip. While you're gone, I'll pick and put up the ripe tomatoes. You just get on that wagon, go to town, and be back before dark."

"That'll be more than ten hours, Alicia," the man replied pleadingly. "Why don't you just go with me like you used to do?"

"John, you know we need every bit of what that garden provides. Until the corn is ready to pick and the steers fattened, one of us has to guard the fences. We can't take any chances."

"Wish that son of mine would hurry up and get born. We need more hands around here."

"John!"

"I know; it could be a girl."

The man put his hand to his wife's round belly and held it there gently. They both felt the movement and smiled at each other.

"Alicia! I won't do it! I can't leave you here with the baby coming, and all alone!"

"John, we need those supplies, and you have to get them. One of us has to stay, and you know it. You're burning daylight. The sooner you're gone, the quicker you're back."

"Okay, I'll go, but I don't like it. Remember, the pistol is on the dry sink, and the loaded Spencer is on the porch. Don't be afraid to shoot like I taught you. Besides, we could use the venison. But don't work too hard."

"Will you just go, John? The baby is not coming for another month. Besides, God will watch over me while you're gone."

The man sighed, bent down, and kissed his wife's mouth. He stroked her cheek with a calloused right hand, then climbed up on the wagon seat. He grabbed the reins, released the brake, and waved goodbye.

Alicia stood watching the wagon move forward. It would take a long time for it to completely disappear into the vast distance.

"That man," she said with a smile. "He sure is a worrier. He acts like bringing a baby into this world is something unusual."

Shaking her head, she willed herself into movement and, picking up her harvesting basket, went to the garden. There were few clouds, and the sky reached endlessly into a vast blue dome. Already the early morning air was growing warm. In a few hours, it would turn hot and be hard to breathe. This was high desert country, and if not for the irrigation from the river, the ground would be powder dry. With water, plants grew big and strong in the hard adobe earth.

Alicia, determined to make the most of the morning's coolness, stepped quickly to the garden and stopped before opening the gate. She held the basket under her arm and stood, looking proudly at their land. Here were three hundred and twenty acres. The Huerfano River ran through the middle of the homestead, and as far as they knew, it never went dry. Near the house was the garden with irrigation ditches flowing into it. On both sides of the river were two eighty-acres of bottomland where grass for hay grew rich and full. This was for the pastured cattle. The new wooden fence stood proud in straight, bold lines.

Nearer to the house and behind the garden grew forty acres of irrigated corn. It would be their cash crop. Come October, and they would harvest it and sell the dry yellow ears, along with ten fat steers. It would bring enough money to help them get through the next year. Without it, they would fail.

Alicia turned from her anxious thoughts and opened the garden gate. She went to the tall tomato plants and began picking. Several ripe fruit had holes pecked in them from hungry birds. The young woman frowned. She chose a damaged tomato and was in the act of tossing it but changed her mind. She wiped it clean on her apron and then, turning it to the opposite side, raised it to her lips and took a big bite. Juice dripped out, and she bent forward, trying to avoid its splatter. The tomato was delicious, and she smiled while she chewed.

How wonderful to enjoy the very first harvest from my own garden, she thought proudly.

Alicia picked until the basket overflowed with tomatoes. There were far too many to boil and can. They had a huge surplus, and many would spoil on the vine or go to waste. Next year, she would plant more corn or potatoes and not lose so much harvest.

Wiping her damp hair from her face with one hand and patting her belly with the other, she spoke softly. "Well, little one, I think we have enough tomatoes to put up for one batch before your daddy gets home. We have to show him he didn't need to worry about us."

She lifted the heavy basket and took it to the pump outside the front door. Setting it on a board that rested on the water trough, Alicia pumped the handle. When the tomatoes were washed, she went into the house and brought back a kettle. This, she filled with round red fruit. Carrying the kettle inside, the young woman placed it to boil on the cast iron stove. Clean canning jars were on the kitchen table, ready to be set into the other large pot of boiling water. It would be an all-day process of cooking the tomatoes down, pouring the sauce into jars, and then screwing on the zinc tops tightly.

For several hours Alicia worked at her task. Every few minutes, she looked anxiously out the window watching for deer. It would be a relief when her husband brought back the dogs he promised to buy. These would be tied on long ropes at night to guard against any wild game or animals that came to feed.

They never thought it would be so bothersome a routine to keep their crops safe. One time when she went to the porch to look, she saw three deer come from the line of cottonwoods near the river. They jumped the fence and began to graze in the hayfield. Alicia took the Spencer, steadied it against the cabin wall, aimed, and fired. The distance was over a hundred yards. She missed, but the deer stopped grazing and looked up nervously. They flicked their tails but didn't leave. Alicia moved the heavy Spencer's trigger lever with difficulty, and the spent bullet was replaced with new. She aimed and fired again, and the deer ran and jumped the fence back into the safety of the trees.

The young woman put the rifle down. This was a long-practiced routine, and without thinking more about it, she went back to preserving the tomatoes. Fifteen minutes later, when she came back out to survey the garden, fences, and hayfield, more than fifty men, women, and children stood in the front yard. Some men were on horseback, the women were on foot, and so were the older children. The babies were in cradles on the backs of mothers, and the toddlers sat high up on loaded travois.

The young woman stared in shocked surprise. She had no idea that Indians were about—and she forced herself not to show fear. They had been told the Utes sometimes traveled the river migrating along the path their people had followed for generations. Still, Alicia and her husband had never seen them before. Now the cabin and new fences stood solidly in their way. This was once their land, and Alicia knew she was the trespasser. These crowded thoughts went suddenly through her mind. She stood staring in disbelief and mounting fear.

"White woman on Peoples' land," said an aged warrior, dismounting.

He left his horse and came forward, stopping in front of the porch. An older Indian woman followed. The warrior was dressed in buckskins, beaded and decorated more than the others. He wore a blanket over his shoulders, an amulet around his neck, and a feather in his long, graying hair. Alicia squinted and raised one hand to shield her eyes. He waited for her to answer.

Alicia gathered her courage and tried to swallow; her throat had suddenly gone dry.

"The gov...," she croaked. "The government gave us this land, and we purchased another section from the farmer who was here before us."

"Last year, we told white man to leave. If he did not, we would burn and take what is ours."

Sudden anger flared in the woman who had worked so hard to raise crops and improve the ranch.

"You will not threaten me!" ordered Alicia. "My husband and I bought this land and worked it, and all that you see is ours! If you want some food and some pickings of the crops, I will share it with you. But this is our home, and we won't leave!"

In her anger, Alicia moved off the porch and towards the warrior. The painted horse behind the Indian snorted and backed up. Indignantly, the chief tightened his blanket around his shoulders.

"No place for woman to speak. Where is man?"

"Gone to town! If you want to talk, it's me you'll have to deal with!"

The Indian grunted. Alicia's anger quickly burned away, and again fear gripped her. She felt the baby inside kick violently in protest, and the suddenness of it made her put her hand protectively to her belly. The chief saw the movement.

"White woman with child. Her man gone?"

"I am fine without him," said Alicia staring at the leader defiantly.

She suddenly felt faint. A violent wrenching twist occurred inside her, and water ran down her legs. In embarrassment and weakness, Alicia backed up and sat down on the porch bench.

Seeing this as a bad omen, the chief turned, mounted

his horse, and rode away from the cabin. He motioned to the members of his band, and, without looking, they turned away.

Three women rushed forward and pushed Alicia inside the building. One laid a blanket on the wooden floor, and another put down an animal skin. Without asking, the three together helped hold Alicia's shoulders. Alicia tried to protest, but a sudden pain gripped her belly. She looked up at the women.

"This," she said. "This is all so..."

"My sisters and I will help you," said the oldest of the three Indian women.

"You will have baby Indian way," one said, pushing Alicia down to a squatting position.

"I don't know what you mean."

"We show you; baby come easier."

Alicia gasped in a sudden contraction, and with it came pain.

"I am chief's wife. Do not be afraid. No harm will come to you."

Alicia closed her eyes and endured another contraction. With them closed, she fought the pain and let a rush of air escape her lungs. Somehow it was easier to do so. The contraction eased and she was able to speak. "I would ask your people to rest the day. I would offer food and some of the crops in the field."

"We could take all, anyway."

Alicia still held her eyes tightly closed against the pain.

"I know, but please, we worked hard, and you see, it would not be here but for us."

"How much would you give?" asked the chief's wife.

Alicia felt dizzy and sick to her stomach. The contraction was lessoning. Alicia opened her eyes, concentrated, and struggled to find the right words.

"Please, take one-tenth of what we have. Crops and cattle, and next year, when you come through here, we will give the same, and the year after that, and every year."

"Whites do not keep their word."

Alicia jerked her head up in anger as she looked at the woman. Pain stabbed at her insides, and she fought it.

"You! I keep my word! Always!"

"My people call me Yellow Leaf." said the Ute wife.

"Yellow Leaf, my name is Alicia, and I do not lie!" she said, staring defiantly.

A slight smile formed on the lips of Yellow Leaf.

"White woman has courage, like the People. You speak truth. We will take no more than one part of ten. Our tribe is tired, thirsty. We rest, eat, gather food. You have baby. Then we leave."

Yellow leaf smiled, and with great dignity, raised a hand in a sign of peace. Then her smile broadened.

"Next year, we do again!"

* * *

Towards evening as the sun was setting, the rumble of the wagon was heard. After a long interval, with a grating of steel tires, thudding horses' hooves and barking dogs, the vehicle pulled into the yard. Alicia sat on colored Indian blankets on the front porch. She held a bundle wrapped in soft deerskin in her arms. From the rafters of the porch hung two dressed-out deer. There was a basket of soft tanned leather clothes for an infant, an Indian baby's cradle, a child's quiver of arrows, and a small bow.

John stood up on the wagon, mouth open, too surprised to speak.

"Come," said Alicia. "Come and meet your son. And while you hold him, let me tell you about the day I had."

JUST SHOOT!

"Are you going to shoot or not?" asked the cowboy tersely.

"I can't; he looks so splendid."

"Just shoot, Miss Helen."

"Oh, he's so magnificently beautiful! How could you ask me to kill such an exquisite animal?"

"I recall, Miss Helen, that you said the meat you ate last night was exceptional."

"Was it from such an animal as that? It did taste rather good."

Bang! The lady's rifle blasted. The buck jumped, ran a few yards, and then nose-dived into the ground, dead.

"Good shot," the cowboy commented dryly.

"In New York, where I come from, there are hunting clubs," said Helen. "Now please, hurry up and clean that thing; it's getting hot out here."

"Yes, Ma'am," replied Frank Beasely, foreman of the Broken Wheel Ranch.

He stood between grudging admiration and frustration as he glanced over at his new boss.

The young lady, Helen Forrester, from New York City,

was the newly arrived heir of this expansive spread. It was 1885, and the fact that she knew nothing of Western life did not inhibit her inquisitiveness. And it was Frank, her uncle's ranch foreman, whom she expected would teach her.

In New York City, Miss Helen Forrester had always been the recipient of all the advantages wealth could provide. Money earned on this very ranch enabled the girl's upbringing—money set up when six-year-old Helen lost her parents. The rancher was Helen's uncle on her father's side, and the aunt who raised her in the big city was her mother's sister. Now that the uncle died, Helen, twenty-one, became the owner and manager of the vast cattle spread. All this to the exasperation of Frank Beasely and the cowboys. They loved the rough owner Hank Forrester but despised the thought of a young city girl taking over.

Frank gutted the deer and tied it onto a packhorse. He mounted and led the animal up to the new owner.

"When can we drive into town with the wagon?" asked Helen. "I've ordered supplies through the mail order catalog. And, you should know there are more of my things being shipped. They should be here by now."

"Holy hot chili peppers!" exclaimed Frank. "You mean you're bringing more stuff out here? That last shipment took three trips with the wagon!"

"Frank!" said Helen authoritatively. "Am I or am I not the boss of this place?"

"Yes, Ma'am, you're the boss…"

"Precisely," said Helen. "You either get used to my ways or…"

"No, Ma'am. I mean yes, Ma'am," sighed Frank.

"Good. I'm glad we understand each other. I'd hate to lose the experienced man my uncle trained."

"Miss Helen…I reckon it was the other way around."

"No need to be impudent."

"Yes, Ma'am," mumbled Frank.

"Oh, and something else," said Miss. Helen. "You order the cowhands to leave my poor maid alone. Why, in the last week, she's had four marriage proposals."

"It's the West," replied Frank. "Women are scarce."

"Well, she's a good French maid, and I don't want to lose her!"

"When it comes to affairs of the heart, that runs a little outside my duties as foreman."

"Well!" exclaimed Helen.

They rode the rest of the way in silence. Frank led the packhorse with the deer, and Helen followed. They traveled across wide-open prairie, and the views were endless. Vast seas of yellow grass, parched by the sun, mingled with the beige ground. Various greens of jumping cholla, prickly pear, pinions, and cedars gave color to the landscape. To the west rose the Rockies nearly three miles high. Even at the end of June, their tops shimmered with snow, and they stretched in a long row, north and south. Nature dwarfed the humans as they traveled over the undulating land.

"It's very pretty, isn't it?" asked the New York lady, quite unexpectedly.

Frank made to spit and then minded his manners.

"Pretty, Ma'am? That's a puny word to describe it. Why, this country's magnificent! Stupendous! Beyond the pale of understanding…"

"Why, Frank! I think you wax poetic!"

"If you live out here, a man can't help it. 'Better a witty fool than a foolish wit.'"

"Now, you quote Shakespeare? Just when I thought…"

"Yes, I know you think we cowboys are a witless uneducated bunch," answered Frank. "But a book occasionally comes to the bunkhouse. Many a storm, or idle time on the trail, or in a line shack gives time to read by lantern or firelight."

"Really?" responded Helen. "How intriguing. Do all cowboys read Shakespeare?"

"Ma'am, they read whatever falls their way. That includes Cooper, Irving, Poe, Dumas, Twain, Shakespeare, the Bible, a newspaper, a magazine, a cookbook, and even a can label. If a long winter keeps a man indoors, there is no telling what bit of reading will fall into a cowpuncher's hands."

"Frank! When we get back, I'll order books be sent to the bunkhouse! We'll build shelves! There's no need for my hands to be uneducated, uncouth…excuse me, Frank. I forget myself."

"'Better three hours too soon than a minute too late,'" Frank quoted Shakespeare. "Perhaps until you learn our ways, Miss Helen, you should not be so quick to judge the men who work for you. They have feelings…"

"And have I stepped on them?" asked Helen.

"Ma'am. Let's say you have been impatient. You act as if they're beneath you. They're smarter than you think. They work in God's country. Why, these fellers just naturally have an eye for beauty. They have strong feelings, even if they can't always express them in educated terms."

"What do you suggest I do?"

"Go slower, learn more. Be less New York. If you want to run this ranch, you are going to have to become one of us."

"I hardly think…"

A tall rider on a magnificent black horse suddenly appeared from behind a thirty-foot wall of rock. Dressed in dark clothing, he cut a striking presence with his swarthy complexion and pencil mustache. His horse was adorned with black saddle and tapaderos. Glints of silver gleamed from the saddle, bridle, and a black hatband.

"Hello, Ma'am," said the stranger touching his hat. "Howdy, Frank."

The foreman dropped the reins of his horse and drew his pistol.

"What are you doing here, Pinter?"

"Why, can't a man ride the range without being drawn down on?"

"You skunk! You were hiding, waiting to waylay us. Miss Helen, keep your distance! This snake is the feller I was trying to tell you about!"

"Frank!" ordered Helen. "Put that pistol away!"

"Ma'am?" asked Frank.

"Put it away, I said!"

Frank, disgusted, reluctantly did as he was told.

"Now introduce us," said Helen.

Frank stared in anger and consternation. He cleared his throat loudly and then made introductions.

"Miss Helen Forrester, meet Howard P. Pintergast."

The man on the black spurred his mount up beside the lady and put out a gloved right hand. She did the same, and they shook.

"Around these parts," continued Frank, "this coyote is known by the name of Pinter, long time enemy of your uncle—suspected for years of being behind our cattle rustling. He's also a low-down land grabber and the man behind every dirty deal in the county."

"Is what you say proven?" asked Helen.

"Proof enough," responded Frank. "He owns the Silver Slipper in town and spends his time gambling. He never loses and always has a gang of bad men around him."

"Thanks for the build-up," said Pinter in a smooth voice. "There's been bad blood between Frank, your cowboys, and me. Judge for yourself, Miss Helen, do I look like a bad man to you?"

Pinter removed his silver-trimmed hat in a flamboyant gesture and revealed smooth gleaming black hair and handsome dark features.

"Frank," said Helen. "Take the horses and your hostility and leave."

"Ma'am?" asked Frank, startled.

"Take the deer and ride to the ranch. I can see it from here and can make my way back."

"You aren't going to be alone with this varmint!" exclaimed Frank. "Why, your uncle would have my sorry hide for the coyotes to chew on if he knew I left you with this reprobate! Why, this mongrel was probably hiding and scoping the ranch for cattle to steal…"

"Enough, Frank!" ordered Helen. "Do as I say!"

Reluctantly the foreman rode up to the packhorse and gathered reins.

"Watch yourself, Miss Helen. He's an oily one, don't be fooled…"

With this declaration, the foreman spurred his horse into a gallop. The packhorse followed in a cloud of dust and pounding hooves.

"Frank doesn't like me," said Pinter in a wide grin and flash of white teeth.

"I can see that," said Helen. "Does he have reason?"

"You be the judge, Miss Forrester," he said and smiled broadly.

Pinter motioned for her to turn her mount up a narrow trail. At a ridge overlooking Broken Wheel Ranch, they halted the horses and sat side-by-side talking. Much of what was said that afternoon on Forrester range would remain between man and woman. After twenty minutes of discussion, Helen learned that Howard P. Pintergast was an educated man with a law degree.

"You mean to say that after all of the time and hard work earning a degree to become an attorney, you did not pursue the profession?" asked Helen with a puzzled look.

"Oh, no, my dear Helen," he said. "I had much better and more profitable endeavors to pursue."

"Mr. Pintergast," exclaimed Helen sharply. "I do not believe our brief acquaintance lends itself to such familiarity as to call me by my given name."

"My apology, Miss Forrester. My hope is that we may become well-acquainted very soon."

Helen studied the handsome face and detected a fleeting smirk. The man continued.

"May I make amends by requesting you accompany me on a buggy ride on Sunday afternoon? There is much of your uncle's ranch I am sure you have not explored."

"I will entertain your request, Mr. Pintergast. You are undoubtedly very busy, as am I. Frank and I must go over the books."

"Please reconsider my invitation. Surely the books can wait," said Pinter in a charming voice reaching for her hand and holding it briefly. "I truly want to get to know you better."

Helen started to recoil but thought better. Handsome or not, something about him did not ring true. She would attempt to learn more about the friction between Pinter, her uncle, and Frank before she came to any conclusions.

Why am I surprised to see an aggressive, domineering man with most likely a hidden agenda here in the West? She thought. I certainly can't expect that type to only live in New York.

"Since you put it that way, Mr. Pintergast," said Helen with a fleeting smile. "I will be honored to accept your offer of a Sunday afternoon ride."

* * *

When Helen Forrester rode up to the stables, Frank and several cowboys armed with rifles were waiting.

"Are you all right, Miss Helen?" asked Frank, obviously worried. "I thought…"

"You were getting ready for trouble?" asked Helen.

“Yes.”

“And you would have used force?”

“Yes, Ma’am. This is the West, and that Pinter is a bad and ruthless man.”

“On Sunday, he is taking me on a picnic and buggy ride,” announced Helen. “And I don’t want any trouble. Do you understand?”

“Ma’am!” exclaimed Frank. “You can’t! He was your uncle’s greatest enemy! Why, he’s rustled this ranch for years; he’s nearly robbed us blind. He’s behind killings, stealing of ranches, cheating at cards. Any dirty dealings in this county, and you can bet Pinter’s behind it!”

“Nevertheless, unless you have definite proof of what you say, I’m going on Sunday.”

“You can’t! And besides, there’s your reputation and the feelings of the hands to consider. They wouldn’t understand...”

“Frank,” interrupted Helen. “Weren’t you going to teach me how to shoot a pistol? Didn’t you say a derringer was effective under the right circumstances?”

“Well, yes,” said Frank. “It’s known as a gamblers’ and ladies’ persuader.”

“Do we have one?” asked Helen.

“Yes, in the office, with your uncle’s other arms.”

“Well, go get it. Teach me how to use it. Now.”

“Yes, Ma’am.”

“Oh, and Frank,” said Miss Helen. “Before Sunday, go through the cattle figures. I want to know the exact number rustled over the years. And be prepared to tell me everything you suspect about the thefts; that includes what you know about Mr. Pintergast."

"Ma'am?" asked Frank, now somewhat bewildered.

"Did you know?" said Helen. "That Pinter was a lawyer trained back east?"

"No," said Frank. "I don't think anyone knows that."

"Well, I do," said Helen. "He told me himself. And Frank, the West is not the only place for ambitious crooks. New York society also has a few."

"Oh," said the foreman. "But I don't..."

"Frank, haven't you ever heard the old expression: 'Keep your friends close, and your enemies closer?'"

"Miss Helen?"

"Tell the hands the boss lady is doing a little investigating of her own. That I don't like losing cattle any more than my uncle did. Tell them to dust off the spyglass and keep their weapons oiled."

"Yes, Ma'am!" said Frank, hurrying off to do as told.

And imagine that, Frank told himself. *I told her not to judge the cowboys. Guess I need to take my own advice.*

* * *

Pintergast drove a fancy buggy into the ranch yard, a gleaming black affair with two matching grays in the harnesses. Cowboys who were not off working turned out to catch a glimpse of the enemy. It ate at the men's innards to see Pinter ride in, a virtual guest. Cowboys spit and glared, many with hands on pistol butts. The boss lady was pulling a slick one and putting herself in danger.

Pinter got out of the contraption and helped Helen aboard. He actually touched her hand and waist. Under different circumstances, it would have been a killing affair, but in this case, the ranch hands could do nothing but stand back and watch. Pinter looked around, smiling, and flashing those white teeth of his out of a sun-darkened face.

"Your men seem upset," said Pintergast, slapping the reins and guiding the buggy out of the yard in a cloud of dust.

"Do they have good reason?" asked Helen.

"Let's just say that a fellow out here has to be tough."

"Are you a tough man, Mister Pintergast?" she asked, staring directly at him.

"Call me Howie. It's a name I prefer."

"Well, Howie?"

"Yes! I'm a tough man. This is a rough place, and let's just say I hold my own and more. I always take advantage of opportunities."

"So you're a taker?" asked Helen, continuing her interrogation.

Pinter laughed.

"Am I detecting hostility, Miss Helen?"

"No, directness. You did not really think me the demure type?"

"I didn't know what to think. That's why I came to meet you. Running into you on the range was a happy coincidence."

"Perhaps. So answer the question, Howie. Are you a man who takes?"

"Let's just say…" laughed Pinter, "that I am a man who does not let a good deal fall through."

"So you're quite successful?"

"Yes, of course, at everything, I set my mind to. Not as rich as these landholdings you have, or the steers and horses you run and sell back east. But I'm getting there."

"You have cattle interests?"

"Indeed. I own ranches, run steers, breed horses, dabble in real estate, own a saloon, a few stores...."

"I see. I'm just learning about my uncle's ranch. I'm not really sure how much stock we…I…have. Nor anything about the income."

"You own fifty thousand acres and run stock on a hundred thousand more of government land. You have one river, one lake, five springs, and dozens of windmills pumping water. You run about thirty-five hundred head of steers and a hundred mustangs. If it was me, given all that water, I'd irrigate, raise more hay, and run a lot more steers."

"You seemed to be well informed about my uncle's ranch."

"It's my job to know what goes on in this county. You see, someday I plan to own it all."

"How ambitious of you. I take it you have already made a lot of enemies along the way?"

"I have. And will make a lot more. And why shouldn't it go to the best man? I see opportunities where others don't."

"And to those who stand up to you?"

"They'll have to fight to keep what they have!" growled Pinter.

"So where do I come into your plans?"

"You're a pretty and educated lady," answered Pinter smoothly. "Not many of those out here in the West. Perhaps you and I can become friends. Enter into a partnership of mutual interest?"

"What do you have in mind?" asked Helen.

"You are direct, aren't you? Well, let's just see how the day progresses."

They drove to the Forrester Lake that Pinter had mentioned. He tied the buggy beneath a silver cottonwood and laid out a blanket for the picnic basket he brought from town. Above them loomed the Wet Mountains. Green pinions and red cedars darkened the slopes all the way to the top. And, by squinting against the backdrop of blue sky, one could see the forms of large Ponderosas growing high up. Long meadows stretched endlessly and lay between giant mountain peaks capped with snow.

"It's magnificent, isn't it?" said Helen. "I've never been here before."

"It's the loveliest spot in the entire county," commented Pinter pointedly. "And you own it."

They were both hungry. In the shade of the cottonwoods, they partook of a lunch of fried chicken, beans, and an apple pie. Dishes, forks, knives, and cloth napkins came with the picnic basket, along with bottles of wine.

"Oh, what a wonderful repast," said the young woman. "This country air makes one so hungry."

"Yes, it does, Helen," said Pinter breathing heavily as he innocently took hold of her hand. "I am so glad we met. Since the very first time I ever saw your photograph, I have been intrigued."

"You saw my picture?" asked the young woman, deftly removing her hand from his grasp.

"Yes, of course. From a New York Magazine. You know, you're in the society pages quite often. We aren't all dullards out here."

"You've been keeping an eye out for me?"

"Yes. I told you, your uncle's ranch is prize holdings, and so are you."

"And you want the ranch?"

"Why yes, of course. I thought you understood that."

"What if I said it is not for sale?" replied Helen quietly.

"There are other ways of getting it," laughed Pinter, again grasping her hand.

The lady abruptly jerked away; there was anger on her face and in her eyes.

"No need to get upset," said Pinter. "I told you, I always get what I want. Ever since I saw your picture, I knew you were the woman for me. Don't play hard to get. I'm just the sort of man you need. One who can run Broken Wheel and look out for your interests."

"I don't think so!" said Helen angrily, and she rose quickly to her feet. "Take me home!"

"Now Helen," said Pinter, also rising and grabbing her wrist. "That's no way to act."

She tried to remove her hand, but Pinter was strong, and she could not free it. The big man towering over her moved forward. Then he slipped his two large arms around her body and strongly squeezed.

"Let me go, you swine!" said Helen.

Pinter laughed.

"Now, how about that kiss I've been waiting so long for!"

He bent down and put his lips to hers. She struggled, but he was much too strong. She was a plaything in his arms, and for the first time, she wondered if she would escape the encounter.

"Let me go!" shouted Helen, finally working her right hand free.

"Never!" answered Pinter with another laugh.

Bang! Helen stood facing the man, derringer in hand. Pinter gasped and backed up, holding a wounded right bicep. Crimson dripped between his fingers.

"Why, you witch! You shot me!"

"Yes! This is a double-barrel, and the next one will go right between your eyes!"

There was the sound of a distant gunshot, and turning around, Pinter caught a glimpse of cowboys on horses, rushing towards the lake. A cloud of dust rose up.

"You have men out here!" accused Pinter.

"Of course!" said Helen, with more confidence. "You didn't think I would go with a snake like you and not bring protection!"

"Why, this was all a plan to get me to talk! You tricked me!"

"It didn't take much cunning!" replied Helen.

"Why, you little…" snarled Pinter stepping forward angrily.

"Careful!" said Helen holding up the derringer and

exposing the twin barrels. "This is a .41 caliber, and it's capable of making a neat round hole in that big conniving forehead of yours!"

Galloping horses came closer. The riders rushed in and skidded to a halt.

"Are you all right, Miss Helen?" shouted Frank. "Guess you were able to handle him."

"Well, I managed," replied Helen. "Now get this con man off the Broken Wheel. The next time we see him, he won't be so lucky."

"All right!" shouted the foreman. "You heard her, Pinter! Get in your buggy and ride!"

"This won't be the last of this!" shouted Pinter, still holding his blood-soaked arm.

"It better be!" exclaimed Helen. "You'll never get this ranch!"

Five other cowboys, all brandishing pistols or rifles, laughed.

"Now git!" shouted Frank, shoving Pinter from the side.

They stood and watched the wounded man dressed in black get aboard the buggy. He was thrown the reins, and a cowboy whacked the rear of one of the grays with a hand. The vehicle lurched to a wild start. Dust flew up behind the wheels as the galloping grays left the shade of the cottonwoods. Helen and her hands watched the buggy for a long time. The new boss mounted a spare horse, and together with her men, she rode back to the ranch.

* * *

With Pinter's shooting, the lady's standing as owner of the Broken Wheel vastly improved. According to the ranch hands, for a New Yorker, Miss Helen had come a long way from being the greenhorn. She might just be worthy of Hank Forrester, and perhaps she wouldn't run the ranch into the ground.

Helen put her plans into action and made changes. The bunkhouse was expanded, and a "reading" room with bookshelves and books was added. When she joined the cook shack for evening meals, the men washed up and minded their manners.

The cowhands learned their boss could be a good sport, and when she started dressing Western and toting a pistol, they were surprised and delighted. The lady could joke and kid with the best of them. At night by lantern light, she participated in a few card games, holding her own, even if she did insist on playing for pennies.

Helen wasn't above adopting the suggestions of her enemy. The men complained but dug ditches and laid pipe. Large acres were irrigated. Cuttings of hay increased, and more fields of grass became available for the horses and steers. A large vegetable garden was set up for the cookie. Prize bulls and Morgan stallions brought from back east began to improve the stock.

Through the next year, Pintergast continued his schemes. Ranchers ran up gambling debts at the Silver Slipper, were rustled, strong-armed, threatened, and pushed off their spreads. Some died. Stores were being purchased in Walsenburg, and a stranglehold applied to goods and services. Pinter ended up with the deeds to the ranches, and he was slowly beginning to acquire and own vast holdings. It seemed that no one was equipped to stop him. He even made a bid to put his own sheriff in office.

Sam, a rider for the Broken Wheel, came to the cook shack for supper and announced that old man Harvey was found dead and that Pinter was offering the widow money for the ranch. The Harvey spread bordered the Broken Wheel.

"That's it!" announced Helen, rising from her meal. "Frank, we have to stop Pinter. Send a rider with my condolences to Mrs. Harvey. See if she needs some help. Tell her if Pinter tries to take her ranch, then I'll make a better offer."

"You heard her, Sam!" said Frank. "Eat up and fork a hoss over there."

"If she asks," said Sam, "what do I offer the widow lady?"

"Five hundred dollars over anything Pinter is paying!" exclaimed Helen to the cowboy.

Helen Forrester wired for more money and used it to purchase the new widow's spread. She found that hard coin had to be on hand to buy a ranch or business, or it would fall into the hands of Pintergast. Slowly, the owner of the Broken Wheel began to find herself involved with owning a dress shop, a gun shop, a saddle making and leather shop, a livery, and several ranches. For cost, these she returned to their previous owners.

Helen consulted with a New York lawyer and was sent an accountant who had worked in many investigative court cases. William Shoemaker arrived by train and set up business in Walsenburg. His assignment was to obtain whatever information he could on Pintergast while fronting as an accountant and bookkeeper.

* * *

A month went by, and at twelve midnight, a buggy drove into the Broken Wheel Ranch yard. Two men hurried from the vehicle and pounded on Helen's front door. It took time, but finally, her maid answered the knock. She woke her mistress, who appeared in a dressing gown. Helen found the accountant, Willy Shoemaker before her, and with him a nervous, fat little man with spectacles.

"What is it?" asked Helen.

"This is Pintergast's bookkeeper," said Willy. "His name is Pee Wee Hickle, and he has important information."

"The two of you go to the foreman's cabin and wake Frank."

There was enough time for Helen to put on a dress and fix her hair. When she came downstairs, the three men were at the front door. She let them in and guided them to the dining room. Two large lamps were lit.

"Well?" asked Helen.

"Tell them, Pee Wee," said Shoemaker.

"I can't. I need something to drink. You tell them."

The maid brought glasses and a pitcher of water. Helen poured and handed the little man the glass.

"I had something stronger in mind," complained Pee Wee.

"That's all you're going to get," responded Helen. "Now talk!"

"I'm Howie's bookkeeper," squeaked Pee Wee, taking a drink and then coughing.

"Howie?" asked Frank.

"You know, Pintergast," said Pee Wee. "That's not his real name. It's Gunter Schwartz. He and I spent time in prison together back in New York."

"For what crime?" demanded Helen.

"For embezzlement of a bank. You see, we both worked there. He was their legal counsel, and..."

"How much time did he get?" interrupted Helen once again.

"Why, he got three years, and I got seven. He blamed most of it on me. Said if I kept my mouth shut at the trial, he would pay me—and a lawyer to get me out sooner. He lied."

"So why are you here?" asked Helen.

"I came west," explained Pee Wee. "After I served my seven, I tried to go straight. Hired on as a bookkeeper up in Denver. Was in a saloon, and in comes Gunter, I mean Pintergast. He recognizes me playing poker and sits in. Afterward, he tells me he has a job. I refused, but he wouldn't take no for an answer. Dragged me down here, and I been working for him the last year."

"So why did you come to see me?" demanded Helen.

"He wants revenge," explained Shoemaker. "Pee Wee knows Pintergast's operation from top to bottom. This bundle of accounting books shows how he's embezzling from the Walsenburg bank and all of his other holdings. It's quite extensive. It's enough to send him to jail."

Helen turned to her foreman.

"If Pintergast were to be arrested, would people come forward to testify?"

"Don't know, boss. Maybe a few might if they thought they would be protected."

"Frank," ordered Helen. "You hold Pee Wee and the books and keep him safe. Tomorrow I'll take the train to Denver with Willy and see the governor. We'll bring the bank books and Pintergast's holdings and show him. We'll ask for federal Marshals."

"Say," said Pee Wee. "I'm not testifying! Gunter will kill me!"

"You stay," said Helen. "You stay so Pintergast and his men can't find you!"

"I won't!" squealed Hickle.

"You will!" said Frank. "And like it!"

"Willy?" asked Helen. "Did anyone see you come out here?"

"I don't think so."

"We'll meet tomorrow early and go to Denver on the morning train. Frank will bring me and the account books to your office at nine sharp. Now go, and don't mention anything about this."

"Yes, Ma'am," answered Shoemaker.

After the accountant left, Pee Wee was placed securely in the bunkhouse. Frank and Helen said goodnight and went to their beds. Early in the morning, Frank Beasely harnessed a buggy and went to the cook-shack for breakfast. Helen Forrester was already there, dressed smartly in a traveling dress and coat. They nodded to each other, drank coffee, ate their food, and walked to the buggy. Helen carried a carpet bag with extra clothing and the accountant's ledgers. Frank helped Helen aboard and taking a seat, the foreman picked up and slapped reins. They went down the long two-rutted trail and got on the road to Walsenburg.

Helen broke the silence. "Frank, do you think the local court will convict him?"

"Perhaps. He's a slippery fellow and won't take anything lying down. Better if the trial's held out of county."

"I'll suggest that. What happens if we fail?" asked Helen.

"Then I'll challenge him to a gunfight and just shoot him down."

"Frank! You can't do that!"

"It's how it's been done for a long time now."

"Those days are over. Times are changing."

"Are they?"

"Yes. Besides, you might get killed or hurt."

"Would you care?" asked Frank.

"Immensely. I couldn't run this ranch without you."

"Is that all?" asked the foreman.

"Do you have feelings for me, Frank?"

"Isn't that a bit abrupt?"

"Yes. Answer the question."

"I might be fond of the boss lady—if I thought I had a chance and it was the right thing to do..."

"It is. And no one will stop you from saying what you think."

"I'm just your foreman. All I got is a hoss, a few guns, and a small bank account."

"That's not what's important to me, Frank. It's the kind of man you are."

"How about we take care of this business with Pinter first?"

"Frank, you're an evasive man. When this is over, I expect you to finish this conversation."

"All right. Are you sure you don't need me as bodyguard in Denver?"

"No, Frank. You stay and take care of the ranch. I'm armed, and I'll make sure Shoemaker is."

They sat mostly in silence the remainder of the two-hour drive to the county seat. Walsenburg was full of cowhands, shoppers, and foreigners getting off the train. Many immigrants were walking the streets. Most would soon be on their way to work in the dangerous coal mines, having no idea what they were in for. At the train station, Shoemaker was waiting. It was crowded, and the accountant stood in line to purchase tickets.

"Do you think it will be that simple to arrest Pinter?" Frank asked Helen.

"I think it depends on just how far Pinter's influence goes," exclaimed Helen. "Between Willy, you, me, the cowboys, and the Governor, we ought to be able to put that crook away for a long time."

* * *

Frank was waiting on the platform when the train pulled into the Walsenburg depot two days later. After the wheels came to a complete stop, Helen appeared on the passenger car's top step. Looking around, she saw Frank and beckoned him forward.

"Howdy, Miss Helen," said the foreman reaching up to take the carpetbag his boss carried.

Instead of giving him her bag, she extended her hand for him to help her down. Once on the platform, the young woman gave her foreman's fingers a gentle squeeze. She seemed to hold on a bit longer than Frank thought necessary.

She hasn't forgotten the conversation, thought Frank. *Her touch was welcoming but wrong time and wrong place.*

"It's good to be back, Frank," she said, looking straight into his eyes.

The ranch foreman met her direct look but felt his face flush and wondered if anyone noticed. Behind Helen came Willie Shoemaker, two U.S. Marshals, along with Governor Benjamin Eaton's right-hand man. The young woman introduced the newcomers to her foreman, and together they walked to the livery to rent horses. They spoke little as the hostler saddled their mounts.

"Miss Forrester," said the governor's man, "Perhaps we're intruding and should take a hotel room or boarding house."

"No, gentleman, you will do nothing of the kind," said Helen. "Broken Wheel has plenty of room and good food. We need secrecy, and we have much to discuss."

The party rode to the ranch, and the maid showed the men their sleeping quarters. That evening at the cook-shack, plans were formed to arrest Pinter. Pee Wee Hickle explained that Pinter would be found in his private office at the Silver Slipper.

"Then that is where we will make the arrest," said one of the marshals. "We will inform the sheriff that his assistance will be required. How many deputies does he have?"

"Three," answered Shoemaker.

"Wait," interrupted Frank. "If you want this raid to be successful, then you'll need to leave the sheriff and his deputies out of this. Nearly everyone in Walsenburg is bought off or intimidated by Pinter and his men. It's too great a risk to trust the local lawmen."

"Unusual," said the other U.S. Marshall. "But, we'll go along with you on this. After all, you brought us the case."

"You do know," said Frank, "Pintergast is not going to be easy to arrest. He has gun-slicks and informants working for him. I'm worried about what was said when you got off the train. That didn't go unnoticed."

"Gentleman," said Helen Forrester. "Frank has a great number of men to choose from. Ones who are willing to fight. I am sure they can be deputized."

"I have ten men standing by," replied the foreman. "I trust everyone of them."

"This is an unusual situation," said one of the marshals. "I counted on the local law to..."

"Sir," said Helen firmly. "The governor and the attorney general said you were to get the job done. We have gone too far to quit now."

"All right then," said the marshal. 'Call your men out, and we'll get them sworn in."

At ten o'clock the next morning, a party of ten deputized

Wagon Wheel Ranch hands and the two U.S. Marshals raided the saloon. Led by Frank Beasely, they entered and took Pinter's men by surprise. Frank moved forward to the office and quickly opened the unlocked door.

Pinter, hearing the outside commotion, rose from his desk, pistol in hand. The foreman shot; and the revolver was struck and knocked to the floor. Pintergast held his injured hand.

"I should shoot you right now," said Frank, "save the court a lot of trouble. "But, I figure a skunk like you won't like prison one bit."

"You don't have nothin' on me," said Pinter.

"Tell that to Pee Wee and the two U.S. Marshals waiting for you. It was Helen Forrester who put this case together. You're going away for a long time."

Pintergast was taken in handcuffs to the train station. Helen stood on the platform watching.

"You hussy," growled Pinter. "No woman is going to best me."

"Oh, really," answered Helen. "It didn't take much to outsmart you. I came to watch you get what you deserve."

"I'll be back," snarled the prisoner, "no jail can hold me."

"Not this time, Mr. Pintergast," said Helen.

The owner of the Broken Wheel Ranch turned around and saw Frank Beasely standing on the platform behind her. Stepping back next to him, she spoke softly.

"Frank, the hands told me what you did. You ran in that office alone. You rescued me, the men, and Broken Wheel again, didn't you?"

"I wasn't going to let him get away," replied Frank.

The foreman and Helen stood on the platform and watched the train depart.

* * *

A few weeks later, the trial moved to Pueblo, and a parade of witnesses came forward to convict. Pinter was given ten years in the Colorado Territorial Correctional Facility, at Canon City, Colorado. Ten days in that notorious correctional facility, Pinter got into a fight with guards and was shot and killed.

The warden's report came back to Broken Wheel Ranch. Pintergast's last words were, "Damn that Forrester woman."

* * *

There was no remorse from anyone when news came of Pintergast's death. The ranch hands' only regret was that Hank Forrester didn't live long enough to see it.

That night a full moon was rising; the bright light illuminated the features of Frank Beasely as he sat on a bench outside his cabin. Helen Forrester approached.

"Mind if I join you, Frank?" asked Helen.

"It's your ranch and your bench."

"Frank, you left early. Ever since the conviction, you've done your best to avoid me."

"Work has kept me busy."

"No, that's not it. You're afraid to talk to me."

"You're my boss, and nothing changes that."

"I told you that doesn't matter. I thought that when the

trial was over, we agreed to talk."

Helen sat on the bench and scooted close. Frank abruptly stood up and walked out from under the cabin's porch into the bright moonlight. Helen looked up and saw her ranch foreman's face. It shone clearly under the full moon, and he was frowning. Both man and woman stared at each other.

"Are you going to say it, or do I?" asked Helen.

"All right then," replied Frank. "I don't have anything to offer you."

"I already said that doesn't matter."

"I know you did. Still..."

"You aren't going to tell me how you feel?"

There was no response from her foreman except a heavy intake of breath. Above both of them flew the broad shadow of an owl. After it passed, it hooted forlornly.

"Frank Beasely, do you care about me?"

"You know I do."

"Then?"

"It'll look bad to your rich friends, being tied to a poor cowboy."

"That's past. You and this ranch are my life now. Brazen or not, I love you. Will you marry me?"

"Not sure how I'll handle a strong woman like you, but since you asked, I reckon."

Helen stood up and came close, and Frank gathered her into his arms. The owl hooted once more off in the distance, and under bright star and moonlight, Frank kissed his boss.

WAR KILLS ALL YOU LOVE

The Union soldiers marched up the road, tired and out of step. Their muskets were resting on their shoulders in haphazard fashion. On horseback, a captain was leading two squads of men, a total of twenty-nine.

"Step lively!" shouted the bearded officer, a young man, staring with weary old-man eyes, and pointing towards a farm. "Five of you search that barn, and the remainder surround it. I don't want one Johnny Reb to escape. You hear me? If one of em' runs, shoot him down!"

The dirty, unkempt soldiers moved lethargically to obey their captain and began to surround the building. A hundred feet away a cabin door opened, and a young woman in a gray dress appeared. She wore a kerchief over blond hair and carried in her right hand a wooden milk bucket. The soldiers stopped all movement to stare. Her worn dress fit her tightly and revealed a full figure. The men made cat-calls and whistled at the unexpected sight. Even the officer was surprised and watched for several seconds before returning his attention to the task at hand.

"Stop that, you fools!" shouted the captain. "Follow your orders!"

In the brief time that the soldiers hesitated, the girl had made her way across the yard, opened a barn door, and disappeared inside. As she entered, she saw movement. She immediately recognized a southern soldier. He carried a rifle, wore a pistol at his side, and stood in tattered clothing.

"Get in the stall with the milk cow!" whispered the young woman.

The Confederate stopped all movement, hesitated in mid-step, and stared at the girl.

"You! Do as I say before they catch you!"

The girl had already opened the stall and was pointing to the floor. She kicked straw away, grabbed at a ring, and a hinged trapdoor opened.

"It's a fruit and storm cellar, and there's a dirt tunnel that opens on a hill. Hurry!"

The hands of man and woman briefly touched as they grasped the hinged door. The soldier began to climb down a crude wooden ladder. In the dim light, both came face to face. The girl frowned. Just then Union soldiers opened the barn door and light flooded into the building. The cellar door closed, and in an instant, the woman kicked straw over the ring. She grabbed a three-cornered stool, sat down next to her milk cow, and began milking. Expertly she pulled on two teats and began to shoot hissing streams into her bucket.

The captain led five of his men into the barn towards the young woman.

"What's your name?" demanded the officer.

"Sally Holt."

"Who else lives with you?"

"No one," answered the girl.

"You mean you run this farm by yourself?"

"Yes."

"Where is the rest of your family?" demanded the captain in a loud voice.

"Dead," answered Sally, continuing to shoot streams of milk. "My father and brothers killed by you yanks, and mother…she couldn't take anymore and…"

"Sergeant!" ordered the captain. "When this girl finishes milking, bring a cup to me, and split the rest with the men. Then take this milk cow and burn the barn. Take what food you can find. I thought I heard a pig, and make sure you get all the chickens. There's a cornfield in the back; pick it clean, and burn it all."

"The cabin, too?" asked the sergeant in a hard sarcastic tone.

"You know Sherman's orders," responded the officer. "Get it done."

Sally Holt rose angrily from her stool and picked up her milk bucket to throw its contents at the captain. The sergeant moved forward, grinning, and jerked the pail from her hands.

"Frank! Russell!" yelled the bucket-wielding sergeant. Two men came forward. "Frank, you finish milking this cow, and Russell, you get this girly out of the barn."

"You can't burn the place!" shouted the young woman, as the soldier grabbed her arm, pulling her towards the wide opening. "What kind of soldiers are you?"

The captain helped Russell drag Sally outside. Her

arms were held tightly as she watched the blue-uniformed men begin a well-practiced routine. Time meant nothing as she saw them run to her cabin and loot it clean of food and personal items. She watched them come out with shirts stuffed with silverware. Others took gunny sacks and disappeared behind the barn. They returned with dead chickens and ears of corn. Then came the milk cow followed by the private named Frank, who carried a full milk bucket. A cupful was brought to the captain, who was back on his horse. Some of the men drank from the bucket while others used stolen cups. Within minutes, the cabin and barn were in flames, and the cornfield behind the burning wooden structures billowed dense white smoke.

"You aren't soldiers," cried the girl. "You're beasts!"

Hearing the farm owner, several of the blue-uniformed men watching the conflagration laughed harshly.

"Lady!" shouted the captain. "No one said war was pretty."

The private, Frank, still held the empty bucket. Feeling sorry for the girl, he turned the container over and placed it upside down on the ground. Russell let go of Sally's arms. Exhausted from her struggle, she sat down. Embittered with rage, dizzy with grief, all she had to her name was being destroyed in yellow flames and acrid smoke. A half-hour passed before Sally Holt finally came to her senses. The cabin and barn were smoking embers, and the cornfield behind, now visible, was burned black. The soldiers were gone.

"I'm sorry, girl," said the southern soldier, now suddenly appearing beside her.

"You fool," said Sally. "I didn't save your life to have you stand out in the open. You should be long gone by now."

"Couldn't leave. Not after what you done for me."

"It doesn't matter," said Sally in a flat, colorless voice. "Nothing matters now."

"Look, my name's Matt, Matt Brady. You come with me. We'll find food, hide in your cellar, and plan what to do next."

"Don't bother with me. You're a soldier. Go find and kill those filthy yanks."

"No."

"No? You say, no?"

"That's right. No," explained Matt. "The war's over, and we lost. There aren't a handful of us left, and those still alive are either prisoners or in hiding."

"If I was a soldier, I'd take up a gun and shoot as many as I could before..."

"I tried that," said Matt. "Honest. There's too many of them."

"And to think I saved your sorry hide," said the girl, suddenly coming to her feet and shouting in anger.

Slinging his rifle over his shoulder, Matt grabbed Sally and put one hand firmly over her mouth. She began to fight back and was surprisingly strong. Squirming herself free, the young woman turned and struck out with both fists. Flailing muscled arms, she got in a flurry of punches. One landed hard on the tattered soldier's chin. Weak from lack of food, Matt Brady found himself falling hard on his rear. He distinctly heard his pants rip, and muttered a curse word under his breath. Coming to his feet, he felt a breeze.

"All right, lady, have it your way. But if you'll calm down, you'll realize you have no choice but to listen to me. Everything you have is gone."

"And don't you think I realize that!" screamed Sally angrily, holding up a clenched fist.

"Suit yourself, come with me or stay here for the Yanks to come back and do more to you," said the man in the tattered gray uniform, and he began walking toward a line of trees.

The girl stood, open-mouthed, and breathing hard. Her fists were still clenched, and she stared at the back of the retreating soldier and saw the wide tear in the center of his trousers. A stretch of yellow-stained underwear met her eyes. With the surprising sight, she smiled. And then, uncontrollably, she began to laugh. The unexpected view, along with her deep-felt grief, made her cry and laugh at the same time. It continued until Matt stopped, turned, and stared in wonder.

"Well?" asked the young Confederate. "What's so darn funny?"

"Your pants," laughed Sally. "They're torn, and what I'm seeing isn't..."

"If you've been in the field as long as I have, you wouldn't be none too clean either."

"No," said Sally, all humor gone from her face. "I suppose not."

"Well, are you coming with me, or are you just going to stand there until something worse happens?" asked the young man.

Matt Brady didn't wait, and once again, he walked away. Sally saw the torn pants and snorted a breath of mirth, and then reluctantly began to follow. At the tree line, the southerner turned towards a sloping hill. Behind a group of bushes was the hole that led into the root cellar. He stooped and disappeared down in the dugout, and Sally followed.

"What are we doing in here?" whispered the girl in the shadow of the dirt cave.

"Do you have anything to sew my pants up with?" asked Matt.

"Is that all you can think of at a time like this?"

"Well, if nothing else, I do have my dignity."

"There's a chest of old clothes near the preserves. Maybe you can find something that fits you."

In the dim light, the two made their way further into the cave until they came to the open cellar. Fumbling in the twilight, Sally found a box of matches and a lantern. She struck a lucifer, lifted the glass, lit, and adjusted the wick. She set the lantern on a shelf with preserves. Matt un-slung his rifle and leaned it against the dirt wall. He located a large wooden trunk, went to his knees, and opened the lid. Inside were various men's clothing, including shirts and several pants. Matt pulled one set of trousers out and came to his feet. Unfolding them, he let them hang and held them up for length against his waist.

"You stay here while I go back and try these on."

"Don't you think you should wash before dressing?" commented Sally.

"Where?" asked Matt.

"There's a well and bucket back by the house. Or what was the house. When it's dark, you can use the soap and a towel that's there. You'd be doing both of us a favor. You smell pretty ripe."

"Look, lady, we was busy and didn't have any chance..."

"Smelling like you do," said Sally soberly, "no wonder we lost the war."

Matt Brady let himself down on a bench in silence and let out a breath of exasperation. They both sat in the flickering light of the lantern and stared at each other. After some time, Matt got up and went to a shelf and pulled down a jar.

"What's this?" he asked.

"Pickles. That's all I had to preserve."

Matt worked the lid off, pulled out one, and took a bite. In the close quiet confines of the cellar, the mingled smell of dry dirt, of an unwashed body, and the dill of the pickle mingled in the air. The chewing and crunching were annoying.

"Want one?" asked Matt.

"How can you eat at a time like this?" asked Sally indignantly.

"Lady, when you've gone without as long as I have, nearly anything tastes..."

"I know! Just keep some space and try not to chew so loudly."

"Of all the people I had to..."

"Well, you're no pleasure, either!" complained Sally.

Again there was silence, except for the repeated biting and crunching of the pickle. When that stopped, both sat and waited out the rest of the day. Before long came heavy breathing and snoring from the exhausted soldier. Sally sat and endured the smell, the breathing sounds, frantically wondering what on earth she was going to do.

Having time to think, the young woman abruptly got up. To the sounds of the soft, uneven breath of the soldier, she went to the trunk and began to rummage through it. She came up with men's clean undergarments, shirts, pants, and shoes. These she laid out on the bench beside her. Then she stood up and put out the lantern. She waited the rest of the day until it began to turn dark, observing the fading light from the far end of the tunnel. When daylight faded, she rose, relit the lantern and shook the Confederate soldier awake.

"It's dark out," said Sally. "I'll lead you to the well, and you can wash up. When you're done, I have fresh underwear and a complete outfit to change into. You might as well get rid of the remnants of your uniform."

"Whose were these?" asked Matt.

"They belonged to my father and two brothers."

There was no response. Sally got up and made her way out of the back of the cave. She carried the clothes and led the way to the well. The soap and towel were still resting on a water trough next to the pump.

"I'll go back now," said Sally. "Throw away those rags you're wearing…I'll wait next to the cave."

When Matthew Brady did not return, she went back down to the cellar. Finding a carpetbag, she packed extra clothing from the trunk. Looking one last time, the young woman found a sack and in it, a dress of her mother's.

Then on top, she placed jars of pickles. When finished, she heard rustling and watched the soldier approach wearing her father's clothing. He was dressed in the canvas jacket that she clearly remembered her father wearing so often. In the lantern light, the young man's washed face shone. The dirt was gone, and his looks were quite pleasing. She smiled, and Matt Brady grinned back, once again exposing even white teeth.

"Well," said Sally. "That's an improvement."

"Thanks. It feels good to be washed and in clean clothes. I almost forgot how good."

"You certainly smell and look better. Now what? "

"I," stated Matthew firmly, "I plan on getting as far out of the south as fast as I can. Figured I'd head west. Once I saw a picture of Denver and the mountains. I been thinking for a long time, that..."

"And how will you live? " interrupted the girl. "Those Yanks are everywhere."

"Reckon I'll do what I did here, help myself."

The girl snickered.

"And that almost didn't turn out so well, now did it?"

Matthew opened his mouth to speak, then stopped. It was some time before he broke the silence.

"Yes, Sally, I am mighty beholden to you," he finally said. "If you hadn't got me into the cellar and kept those men distracted, I wouldn't be here now. Matter of fact, I don't think you would have fared so well either if they found out you helped me. You saved my life."

"Reckon you being young and all, like my brothers, and fighting for Lee, I couldn't do anything different.

They would have taken and burned everything anyway, no matter what."

"We'd best be moving out now. More of them troops are likely to be through here come daylight," said Matthew. "You have kinfolk nearby who will take you in? I can help you get there afore heading west, won't be no bother."

"No bother?" Sally bristled. "No, sir, don't you be worrying about me being a bother. You just get going now. I can take care of myself."

"Didn't mean to make you angry, but you can't be traipsing across the country with me—I can't take care of you," said Matthew. "Besides, it wouldn't be safe, and it wouldn't be decent. I wasn't raised that way. Now, do you, or do you not have kinfolk I can leave you with?"

Sally turned to the man and responded angrily.

"No, I don't have any kinfolk! None! My parents and brothers are gone. My home is gone! I don't have one living creature on this earth who cares a hoot and holler about me. It seems time and this war has taken everything I love."

The girl turned to the man and spoke more softly—this time with determination and strength in her voice.

"But, I do have one thing that you don't. I have understanding of this part of the country. My ma was sickly most of my growing up, and I spent a lot of time with my brothers as they hunted and fished. I know every brook and trail from here to the state line, and I can take care of myself."

Sally picked up her carpetbag and started walking to the tunnel exit. Matthew stood in silence, mouth open, watching this fierce young woman as she stomped away. She reached the opening and stopped.

"Now, Matthew," she called. "If you just happen to want my help to get out of these woods, you are welcome to come with me. Just maybe I can keep you alive, if you let me."

The young man grabbed his rifle, grinned, and rushed to catch up. They walked in silence with Sally leading. They skirted around bogs and slunk low along burned cotton fields. At daylight, they came to a ravine that afforded protection from being seen. Matt spread out a torn blanket that he had tightly rolled in his pack, and they both sat down, shoulder's and thighs touching.

"We could get married," said Matt Brady, flashing a look at Sally.

Turning his gaze to the ground, his clean face showing a red tinge. There was nothing but silence and the sound of their breathing. When Matthew finally dared to look up, he saw the serious expression upon Sally Holt's face, but she didn't say a word.

"I...I been a lot of things in my life," explained Matthew, "but I was never a cad. If you think it's not honorable for us to travel together..."

"Matthew," declared Sally, "I don't know a thing about you. I'm not saying I would, or I wouldn't marry you, but before I'd even think about it, I have to know you a lot better."

"That seems fair."

"There is one thing I know," laughed Sally mischievously.

"Yes?" asked Matthew.

"I already saw much more than a southern lady ought to have..."

They both laughed.

After talking softly, they spent the remainder of the day resting in the ravine.

At dusk, Matthew Brady picked up his rifle and the carpetbag. He took Sally's hand to pull her up out of the hollow. Together, they made their way into the dark. Shouldering the rifle and carrying the bag in his left hand, the former soldier again reached for Sally's hand. She didn't pull it away. It felt good. Together, under dim starlight, they walked a narrow trail, heading west.

THE OLD MAN AND THE KID

Mountain Jack was tough as rawhide and, despite his sixty-plus years, was still strong with ropey muscles and stringy sinews. He could out-walk, out-fight, and out-shoot men half his age. But the man was no match for the Springfield rifle and the .45 bullet that took him on the side of the head and blew him off Raton Pass road. Unconscious, he tumbled head-over-heels more than forty-five feet, into a wet, muddy hole. The five killers were too lazy to go down and check out their latest victim.

"What the blazes did you go and do a thing like that for, Dick?" asked the leader of the gang.

"Heck, Johnny, my rifle has been shooting a bit to the right lately," growled the outlaw. "I just wanted to check out my sights."

"Well," commented Billy, the youngest of the lot, pulling on his peach-fuzz mustache. "I ain't climbing down that hole just to check out some old geezer."

"Yeah," said a fourth bearded outlaw, looking down the steep incline. "Take a mite of effort to climb in and out of there."

"Well, let it be then," gruffly commented the leader.

"We at least got a hundred in gold and a couple weeks supply of food and ammunition off that last immigrant wagon."

The five men packed the stolen supplies on the confiscated mules hidden in the pines and headed out. They left behind in a depression, the smashed and thoroughly searched wagon. The man and his wife's bodies were more easily disposed of by throwing them down the same rocky cliff off the main trail.

* * *

Mountain Jack awoke to find the side of his face lying in cold, wet mud, and the lower half of his body immersed in water. His mouth was open, and he raised his pounding head up to spit out some of the adobe clay. It was the mud that saved his life from the steep fall. Another few feet over was a standing pond of water, and had his head, instead of his legs, landed in it, he would have drowned.

"Darn bushwhackers," mumbled Jack. "If I get out of this, I'll hunt 'em down to a man."

"Are you all right, Mister?" came the call of a young voice.

"Give me a minute to find out, young'un," declared Jack, stiffly rising up. "Haven't tried all my parts yet."

"I saw them shoot you, Mister," said a youth, dressed in a buckskin-fringed jacket and corduroy pants. A light caliber rifle rested across a shoulder. "Thought you were dead, sure. You're still bleeding a might from the side of your head."

"Well, darn-nation boy, why didn't you give me some warning of those side-winders?"

"Couldn't. I was hiding too close to 'em. But I saw them, and I won't forget. The youngest was named Billy, then there was a Dick, two others, and the leader they called Johnny. They were the filthiest and meanest fellows I ever saw."

Jack felt the side of his head, and it hurt to touch it. His hand came away with gore.

"Here," groaned Jack. "You help me tie this up with my neckerchief."

Gingerly, the youth came forward, took the proffered cloth, and tied the bandanna tightly around the head wound with surprising gentleness. There was something different about this lad, and once the boy backed up, Jack studied him out of the corners of his eyes.

"What's your name? And what you doing out here alone?"

"Pa called me Franky, and—no—I wasn't alone. Those same devils shot and killed my parents," explained the youth. "I was off the trail hunting game and away from the wagon when they were bushwhacked. By the time I got back, it was all over. I hid in the brush and watched them smash up the wagon, steal the supplies. They threw my…"

The voice broke, and Jack, now staring intently, heard the softer pitch, and looking closely at the face, started to wonder about the youth.

"Kid, call me Jack. It's a hard place out here. Sorry you had to see that. You tell me where, and if I can, I'll bury them decent."

The old man finally stood to his feet and began to brush off the mud. Confused by the demeanor of this youth, Jack kept his suspicions to himself. He wasn't sure what this kid was—a boy or a girl.

When his head cleared, the mountain man looked around, and with difficulty, located his powder horn and bag of shot.

"Think you can mosey up the hill and see if you can catch sight of my Hawkins .50?" Jack asked. "Sure hope those skunks didn't get their hands on that."

The youth nodded and disappeared up the trail. Jack stumbled to the edge of the water and dragged his pack away. Dizzily he carried the items to a large rock and sat down. The kid found and returned with the old man's rifle.

"Need to get my balance, Franky. That bullet sure cracked my noggin."

"Mister, if we're going to climb back up, there's an easier way going around the pond and following a game trail I found."

"You betcha. Give me a couple minutes here to stop the spinning."

Suddenly Jack felt sick to his stomach, and everything that was left in it came up. It hurt his head something awful, and then he passed out. The youth ran to the old man but was too late to catch him when he fell off the rock. Franky turned Jack over, his body adjusted, so he lay flat and face up. Searching the pack, the youth found a small canteen and poured half its contents over the oldster's wrinkled face. There was no change, except that the water washed off some of the smelly spittle.

Jack lay unconscious. His breathing was shallow. He was too heavy to move, so the youth emptied the pack out on the ground and proceeded to do all that could be done. A damp wool blanket was found to cover the man. The rest of the meager supplies were searched. There was little else except pieces of meat wrapped in leather, a tin plate, and cooking supplies. The kid studied the oldster dressed in stained buckskins. He looked like what he was, an old mountain man.

Franky stood watch through the afternoon. The weather was changing, clouds drifting in over the mountain. Finally, the youth climbed up out of the hole following the game trail and stood guard with rifle in hand. High up, buzzards floated and circled. A light breeze blew and shook the green grass, shrubs, pinion, and larger pine trees. Now and then, a hawk screamed, and the lonely howl of a wolf echoed against high stone crags. It was a beautiful mountain pass, but to Franky, the exquisite scene was lost to dark thoughts. The idea of dead parents, lying torn and broken, somewhere close, was deeply disturbing. The kid brushed away tears.

They're worse than animals, thought the youth. *They gave no warning and shot them off the wagon in cold blood. How many others have they killed? I heard them, all five of them talking and laughing. So help me, they are going to pay for killin' ma and pa. Maybe the old mountain man will die too, just because I was too much of a coward to warn him.*

Franky stood careful guard over the old man through the afternoon. Remorse and regret of not shooting even one of the killers when there was a chance, tortured the youth.

I'll track and hunt them down if it's the last thing I ever do.

In late afternoon, Franky climbed down the cliff and checked on the man. The oldster was still breathing slow, shallow breaths. He didn't look like he was going to awaken any time soon. It was fall; the wind began to pick up, and with it came cold clouds. It was like a wet blanket of fog at that height on the mountain, and it chilled a body to the bone. Franky had no choice but to make a better camp, and once the decision was made, work began in earnest.

The youth looked around, picked out a spot under two pines, and began to gather sticks and boughs. A lean-to took shape. The covering of thick branches was wide enough to fit a bedroll and two bodies. This took several hours of work. Taking the huge bowie knife from the mountain man's thigh, the kid used it to cut rope and string to secure the lean-to. It was now dense enough to keep water off in a storm. A fire was built facing the shelter and backed with rocks.

With some difficulty, Franky managed to drag the old man to the shelter and place him inside. The last task before dark was to gather enough wood to keep the fire going through the night. It took time to find old logs and branches, break them up, and carry them back to the camp. The youth reluctantly entered the shelter. Freezing, the kid shared the single wool blanket.

During the night, Franky got up and added more fuel to the fire. Two smaller logs, their ends facing each other, fed the main part of the fire. When they burned down, the remainder was continually shoved forward. One time, in the middle of the night, hunger pains overcame tiredness. Finding the meat, the youth cut the chunks into thin strips and put them on sticks next to the fire to cook. The kid ate half and kept the remainder for morning.

Franky awoke to a cold wind that shifted and blew directly into the shelter. Sometime in the early morning, the fire had burned down. All that remained was a waft of smoke, emitting from white ashes. The youth stood up, poked at the fire, and got it going by adding bits of bark and twigs. Once it was blazing, Franky chewed on a cold strip of steak and then got the idea to cut the rest up into pieces and make a broth.

If the old man didn't wake up soon, maybe warm liquid could be spooned into him. That bullet crease to the skull must be washed and taken care of. The muddy pond the old man fell onto was part of a stream flowing into the valley. It ran right past their camp. It was a simple matter to get fresh water by filling the canteen.

Caring for the frontiersman and keeping the fire going, the teen got through the next day and following night. When Jack finally did awake on the morning of the third day, it was under the wool blanket and in the relative warmth of the shelter. A banked fire burned in the fire-pit.

The mountain man rose slowly; the extreme pain of a headache made him move cautiously. Jack looked around inside his shelter and grimaced approval. The youth who had cared for him was nowhere to be seen. The oldster sat up, felt for his rifle, finding it cleaned and apparently loaded. A full canteen was beside him. He removed the stopper and took a long drink. This kid, he or she, was no greenhorn. With that thought, Jack, still feeling weak, lay back down and quickly fell into a deep sleep.

The youth was on a hunt. The last of the cooked meat was gone, and game had to be found. At the same time, a lookout for the bushwhackers must be kept. Franky hunted most of the morning. There were elk, mule and whitetail deer, and other game in these mountains. Still, making a shot in the vicinity of the robbers wasn't the best of ideas. The kid saw no animals. In a jacket pocket, the youth did have hooks and line. The small stream might have trout in it. Franky cut and made a pine pole and wrapped the line around the tip. Turning over rocks, bait was found. Fishing the deeper holes, five small trout were caught and cleaned.

Jack awoke to the smell of cooking fish.

"Say," called out the old man from the recesses of the shelter. "Could you throw me one of those? I'm starved."

"You're awake!" answered the startled youth.

"Yup! But my head feels no better. What did you do to me?"

"Nothin', but let you sleep."

"Huh. Mighty fine shelter, kid. And, I seem to remember someone fooling with my head and trying to choke me with broth. Was that you?"

"Maybe."

"Maybe—nothing! Well, you done a good job. Now give me one of those fish!"

Jack ate sitting up, and then crawled out of the shelter.

He broke into a sweat, and when he tried to stand up, went weak in the knees. His head hurt him something awful, and he was still dizzy. They stayed three more days; all the time, Franky provided food and water until the mountain man was able to stand and get around.

On the morning of the sixth day, Jack rose early and began to make his pack. While he stoked the fire, he cut off a steak from a haunch of venison hanging down from one of the pine trees. The kid had brought the deer meat in, the night before. The old man jabbed several steaks on clean whittled sticks, drove them in the ground next to the fire to cook. He began to think about his young companion, who was still asleep inside the shelter.

Nope, this Franky is no greenhorn. The way the shelter and reflecting fire is arranged, not even I could do better. Did all this here for me after his parents were murdered. There's nothin' weak about this youngster—no sir, nothin' weak at all.

"Get up," called Jack. "You been lazing around long enough."

"Watch your mouth, old man," responded the youth. "It's you that's been doing the sleeping."

Jack snorted and grinned back at the kid's face coming out of the dark shelter.

"Come on, let's git movin'."

"Are you up to it?"

"Don't you be worrying about me."

"Can I eat first?"

"Steaks all ready. Chew it up fast, and we'll go."

"Where?"

"I promised to bury your folks and put a marker over 'em."

"How you going to climb further down the valley with a cracked head?"

"You let me worry about that. Eat up, and then show me where they are."

The old man kept his word. They climbed along the deep hollow, leaving the camp just the way it was. If the killers came back, let them worry about who made it.

It took most of the day for Jack to find and bury the bodies. Having a good idea of what he would find, the mountain man told the kid to stay behind. Coyotes, and other animals had done their work, and the bones were chewed and scattered. Digging a hole in the earth with a stick and his hands, the old man covered the remains with dirt. Still weak, he called the youth to help cover the graves with stones. When they were finished, they made markers of wood. With a determined and anguished face, Franky carved into a tree: Martha and James Fuller, Killed by thieves, October 30, 1868.

"Reckon you have your reasons, but I figure you're holdin' back? What's your real handle?" asked Jack.

There was a long silence as the young person stood wiping at the moisture that streaked red cheeks.

"Frances," answered the girl through tear-stained eyes. "Pa always called me Franky cause he was hopin' for a son when I came along."

"Well, Franky, you're sure no greenhorn."

"Back in Ohio, Dad ran a trap line. Taught me to hunt

and fish. Pa said I made the best girl-son ever. When he talked Ma into coming out here to homestead, he said I'd better dress like a boy."

"Franky, I'm sorry it came to this."

"Me, too."

"Come on. I'll take you into town. Trinidad lies down the mountain."

"I know, we just came from there. I'm not going."

"Kid, you can't stay with me—especially you being a girl," said the old man.

"What's that have to do with it? And just where you going when you get rid of me?" demanded Franky.

"After them bushwhackers."

"Then there's nothing you can say that'll stop me," she snarled. "I was hoping you'd help me get those killers. Even if you didn't, I vowed a few days ago up on that ridge that if it was the last thing I ever did, I'd finish them."

"Just how old are you?" asked Jack.

"I'm thirteen, going on fourteen."

"You sayin' you'd do such a fool thing as go after them alone?"

"Bet your boots, I would."

"You wouldn't get but one or two before the rest killed you."

"Doesn't matter."

Jack studied the determined expression on the face of the kid.

"I can't keep no girl. I have to take you to the sheriff."

"I won't stay. I'm not living in no town and be someone's servant. I just won't do it, so don't even try."

"Well, kid," said Jack. "I don't have to ask whether or not you can use that rifle. What distance can it shoot?"

"Hundred yards, sure."

"Okay, Franky. I'll think on it, but for now, you come with me."

"It's not up to you, old man."

Jack snorted. "Call me Jack, kid. Call me Jack."

* * *

So began the strange friendship of Franky Fuller and old man, Mountain Jack.

"You know, girl," said Jack, as they sat talking in his small shack back in the foothills. "The law in Trinidad ain't gonna act kindly to anyone takin' matters into their own hands. Fact is, some of those wearing badges might be sympathetic to them bushwhackers."

"No matter," said Franky. "We're going to find those killers and make them pay for what they did. If you don't want to help, then I'll do it myself."

"Wait a minute. I didn't say nothing about not helping. I just don't like the thought of a youngster like you getting hurt."

"Jack, they killed my parents. With or without you, I'm going to stop those fellers from murdering anyone else."

"You do know the law, or a posse could go after us. I'd hate to see you swinging by a rope."

"I told you, nothing's going to stop me."

"Then we'll have to work out a darn good plan."

The man set his cup on the table and stood up. Putting both of his massive gnarled hands on the girl's shoulders,

Jack looked Franky straight in the eyes.

"Kid, let's agree on one thing. If'n we can figure out a way to take those killers in, legal-like, then that's what we'll do. We'll at least give them a chance to give up. Can you go along with that?"

Franky frowned, "You and I both know they don't deserve no trial. Besides, they'd find some sure way to get off."

"If you don't agree to do it my way," said Jack, "I won't be helping."

"All right, old man, but I don't like it."

* * *

The two worked together. It took a week, but they found the outlaws' camp on the other side of Fisher's Peak. It was an isolated place where no one went. The five scavengers had a cabin, perched on a peak, hidden by thick pines, with vast views of the surrounding valleys.

Their horses were kept in a dilapidated shed of mismatched boards, with a roof slanted down on one side. The cabin the men lived in wasn't much better. It was a crude affair where both sides of the roof leaned crookedly, patched with bits of wood and tin. There were two windows, one front and back, and one door. A crooked and bent chimney pipe poked out one end of the roof.

"Looky here, Franky," said Jack. "Those men are dead shots and stone-cold killers. We got to think on this here before we make our move. Now that we know where they are, we're in no hurry."

"But Jack, they might make another raid, like they did

on my folks. I can't let that happen."

"Kid, you won't help nobody if you're dead. Barge in on them, and that's exactly what you'll be. We got to be twice as smart and twice as careful. I promise you, we'll get them for what they done. If we can take them in, we will."

Jack and Franky made a cold camp some distance from the outlaws. There they talked about what might work.

"In the morning, we could stop up their chimney and smoke them out," said Franky.

"And what noise would you make gittin' up there?" commented Jack.

"We could wing them one at a time coming out of the cabin."

"No, these are experienced killers. You might git one or two, but the remaining three would find some way to sneak away, track us down, and kill us."

"Then what do we do?"

"I don't know. We got to..."

"If only we had some way to get them drunk. Maybe we could…"

"That's it!" said Jack. "Get them cockeyed, and we might have a chance to actually tie them up and take them in."

"But how?"

"I'm thinkin' on it."

To plan, Jack led the girl back to his cabin on the other side of Fishers Peak.

Bits of broken wagons lay all along the pass. Jack got the idea to make a hand cart from the debris. Then, on his own, he went down the mountain and purchased cheap homemade liquor from a Mexican still. He bought a burro and packed the brew up to the cabin. Together, Franny and Jack loaded the cart with a small barrel and three bottles. With effort, they dragged it near the thieves' hideout. Deliberately wrecking one wheel of the cart on a flat area far below the outlaw's camp, they proceeded to shout, yell, and discharge a rifle. Before leaving, Jack broke the neck of one of the bottles, and most of the contents spilled to the ground. Then they hid.

The noise caused two of the outlaws to investigate. The thieves took no chances. Using cover of trees, they cautiously approached. They took their time, and it wasn't until dusk before they came to the broken cart.

"Looky there, Johnny," said Dick, wiping his dripping nose with the back of his filthy shirt sleeve. "That there looks like liquor."

Poking a broken bottle with the barrel of his rifle, Johnny sniffed and looked around. Bending down, he picked up the remains of the bottle. Sticking a finger in the liquid, he tasted it.

"Glory be, sure is! Powerful strong, too!"

"Looks like some fellers were dragging this here cart, and it broke," said Dick.

"You think? But what were they doing way over here and clean off the pass?"

"Don't know," said Dick.

"Peculiar," said Johnny.

The older bearded outlaw picked up an intact bottle and managed to uncork it. He took a sip, and it scorched all the way down his throat. When it hit his stomach, it burned and made a warm glow.

"You think it's poison?" asked Dick.

"Nawww. I reckon those fellers that brought this cart just couldn't carry it all and left this behind. Dick, I'll take the two bottles and your rifle. You go ahead and carry that keg."

"Why do I have to do the heavy lifting, Johnny? Youse stronger than me."

"'Cause I'm your better, boy, and you knows it. Now fetch!"

Dick did as he was told and lifted the small keg. Franky and Jack watched the two thieves carry the fiery homemade brew up the mountain.

After a time, Jack laughed. "I never tasted that poison. I should have. Bet it's 80 proof or better."

"What does that mean?" asked Franky.

"40 percent alcohol, lassy. Enough to get any man dead drunk and in a hurry."

"What do we do next?"

"Well, it's getting dark. We can wait until morning. Them being sick and hungover might give us the edge."

All that night, Franky and Jack listened near the cabin and heard the thieves carry on as they drank until stupefied. Towards morning, Billy fought Johnny, the leader. The youngest outlaw, with a knife in his belly, came out the front door, fell, and died.

"Guess that's one we won't have to worry about," whispered Jack.

To complete their plan, Franky climbed to the back of

the cabin to guard the single window. The mountain man took a position in front, where he could watch the other one and the door. At daylight, Jack called out. They would give the outlaws a chance to surrender.

"Hey, you, the cabin!" he shouted .

There was no response. Despite repeating several loud calls, the four killers inside the cabin remained asleep. Jack fired a shot high up through the window and shouted once more.

"Come out with your hands raised!"

Johnny was the first to awaken when glass landed on his face. Groggily he got up; his head and stomach pained him. The thief searched for his rifle and then went to the broken window. He scanned the sloping area before him and saw an old man hiding behind a clump of boulders. The outlaw aimed, fired, and missed. His bullet struck the rock in front of where Jack was hiding.

From then on, it was a prolonged fire-fight as the other three outlaws slowly came awake and picked up their rifles. Shots were sporadic as black powder rifles were loaded and fired.

"Give it up," shouted Jack. "You don't have a chance."

The answer was a rifle blast from the broken window.

The cabin was badly built, and bullets carefully aimed by Jack found their way through cracks in the door and chinks in the wooden logs. The rifle fire continued all day long. By evening, three of the outlaws were dead, killed by the old man.

The leader, Johnny, survived by hiding behind dead bodies. He tried to sneak out through the back window.

“Stop right there!”ordered Franky.

Johnny pointed his weapon toward the voice. Franky aimed her rifle, pulled the trigger, and did not miss. The five outlaws would pillage and kill no more.

Leaving the bodies as they lay, Jack and the girl returned to the old man’s cabin.

“Now, young lady, we did what needed to be done. Suppose it’s time for you to go to Trinidad and get some schoolin’. Maybe someday you might even find a young feller.”

“Not on your life. I’m not going to live in some crowded town. Besides, someone has to look out for you, old man.”

For once, Jack didn’t respond; he just smiled.

KATY BENNETT

Katy Bennett might have had a chance to be raised as a normal girl had her mother not died in childbirth and her father not been shot down in the prime of his life. The sheriff, finding the precocious little toddler in town without a parent, against his better judgment, had no choice but to seek out her only living relative, Uncle Lefty Bennett. Now, Lefty was a notorious fellow about the town of Pueblo. He had tried his hand at many activities around the dusty little village. Like Katy's father, who died stopping a bank robbery in town, he was handy with a six-gun. Among the many occupations Lefty had tried were stagecoach guard, deputy sheriff, Wells Fargo agent, train guard, and cowhand.

Lefty Bennett wasn't much for sticking with one job. He was a famously gruff fellow, who often spoke his mind, and just naturally defied authority. Working as a ranch hand, Lefty had the effrontery to ask the boss for an advance on his monthly wage.

"What you want the money for?" asked Evans, the ranch owner.

"Well, I got a hankering for a better outfit."

"What fur?"

"Some of the boys say I look like a scarecrow, and I need to buy new duds, get a haircut, and get a fancy bath in town. They say I smell might ripe downwind."

"You look all right to me," said the rancher. "So what if your clothes are patched, and your boots are down-at-heel? I don't need one of my hands smelling like lilacs, neither. I reckon I won't lend the money, Lefty."

"Well then, boss, I reckon you can shove this here job."

"That ain't no way to act!" shouted the rancher. "You get off my place!"

"Was already leaving."

"Don't expect no recommendation neither. When I get done talking, no one will hire you here about!"

"You forgettin' the time those men tried to rob you coming home with the supply wagon from town? And I come along and put a stop to it? Those boys were playing rough, and we shot it out, and you said I had a job for life."

"I ain't forgettin', but Lefty, you go too far…a man can't just be giving advances for tomfoolery."

"If that's the way you feel about it, I'll pull freight."

"Lefty, when are you gonna ever settle down?"

"When I'm too old to move and too feeble to care."

At that moment, Sheriff Langdon came from town, carrying the toddler Katy Bennett up front in the saddle.

"What in tarnation?" asked Evans, seeing the unaccustomed sight.

"How's come you got my niece?" asked Lefty, recognizing his brother's daughter.

"Sorry to tell you, Lefty, but your brother's dead,"

explained Sheriff Langdon. “He got kilt stopping a bank robbery in town. He brought Katy for Saturday shopping, and I found her standing over her dead daddy. Now I got to figuring, and being that you’re her only living relative…”

“Who shot Kenny?” asked the angry brother. “Did you get those fellers? Just tell me what direction they took, and I’ll…”

“There were three of them, Lefty, and your brother was right in front of the bank when they come piling out, money in hand. Kenny stood his ground and shot it out. There was a lot of fireworks, and it was over real fast. Your brother got all three before…”

“Who were they?”

“One of ‘em was Smiley Laycock.”

“That crud…sure he’s dead?”

“Shot between the eyes,” said the sheriff.

“Good!” said Lefty. “Say, he’s the brother of that Baldy Laycock, card shark and saloon owner. Did you go after him?”

“Had a talk with him,” said Langdon. “Told him he was being watched. Can’t pin nothin’ on him since your brother did too good of a job.”

“Someday that hombre and me are gonna…”

“You leave that to the law,” retorted the sheriff. “Had my eye on Laycock a long time. One of these days, he’ll trip up, and we’ll prove he’s behind the rustling and robbing.”

“You know he put his brother up to rob the bank, and now Kenny’s dead.”

“That brings me full circle,” interrupted the lawman. “Little Katy here needs a home, and you’re her father’s brother, and I brought her out to you."

"I ain't no feller to raise no infant," said Lefty.

"I figured you'd see it that way," replied the sheriff. "Might be best at that. I asked around, and the Sullivan family said they would take her."

"They already got a passel of kids!" retorted Lefty.

"That's why I figure Katy would fit right in, never notice one more."

At that moment, Katy's blonde hair blew lightly in the wind. She sat up on the sheriff's saddle looking as lovely a child as God ever made. Then she thrust out her arms toward her father's brother.

"Uncle!"

Silence prevailed for a time. All that was heard was the rustling of hot wind. Katy repeated the word and once again extended her arms.

"I'll take her," said Lefty, surprise showing on his face as well as those of the rancher and the sheriff.

The lawman handed the girl to the uncle.

"Now, what in tarnation are you going to do with that little girl?" demanded Rancher Evans after the sheriff departed.

"Well, I figure I'll take over her daddy's ranch. But now I'll need a bigger loan than just for a set of duds. Evans, could you lend a man and his niece an advance? Say…three months salary?"

"And if you're working on another place, how in land's sake can you stand there and call it an advance?" asked the disturbed rancher.

"Well then, a loan?"

"I ain't no bank!" declared Evans.

Lefty, still holding little Katy, followed Evans up onto the rancher's long porch. The child squirmed in his arms to be set free. He let her down. Without either man noticing, the little girl quickly climbed down steps backward, came to her feet, and ran for the legs of Lefty's mustang, which was tied to the railing. The child grabbed the horse's leg and the cayuse nickered in alarm. It stepped back nervously, but Katy held on. Both the rancher and Lefty turned to see the child fall and go to all fours under the belly of the horse. Four heavy hooves stepped forward and barely missed the young child's head, arms, legs, and torso.

"Holy smoke!" exclaimed Rancher Evans.

Lefty dove off the porch and under the horse. One hoof came down hard on the man's leg. He yelled out in pain as he scooped up the toddler in his arms and rolled out from beneath the thousand-pound beast.

"How in blazes are you going to raise that child, Lefty?" questioned the rancher. "Why, you can't even keep her out of harm's way for one minute?"

"Are you going to lend me the money or not!" exclaimed Lefty Bennett in a stentorian voice.

Lefty glared fiercely as he held Katy with his right arm while rubbing his sore leg with his other hand. Reluctantly, Rancher Evans sighed, reached for the inside of his vest, and pulled out a large fat wallet.

* * *

You might say that Sheriff Langdon and Rancher Evans didn't exactly trust Lefty Bennett to the raising of little Katy. Or, one might look at it another way—they took concern and then eventually a real liking to the little girl. And because of a growing emotional attachment, the two more responsible men ended up becoming surrogate uncles and helped in the raising up of Katy Bennett. Or at least they tried. The little girl loved all three of her uncles. On occasion, when Lefty took Katy to town with him, he would stop by the jail where Sheriff Langdon and sometimes Rancher Evans might be having a cup of coffee. The sheriff made it a special point of putting her up on his saddle with him and making his rounds showing Katy off .

Both men, sheriff and rancher, became closer friends in their endeavor to help raise Katy up a proper girl. But their gentler ways did little to persuade Lefty Bennett's rough parenting. As years past, both men visited often and were first-hand witnesses to Bennett's gruff behavior.

"Katy," they heard Lefty say to his niece. "Now you go in that barn and muck out the milch cow's stall. When you're done with that, use the wheelbarrow and haul the stuff to the pile back of the barn. Then milk Petunia and bring the bucket to your good uncle. I got a hankering for some of the creamy milch in my coffee!"

"Lefty!" said Sheriff Langdon coming down off his horse. "You're raising her up to be a boy. That works not fittin' for no gal!"

Rancher Evans rode in, got down, tied his cayuse to the rail, and joined the two men on the cabin's front porch. There were three chairs, and a table crowded there. Come

Friday evenings, the three men took to drinking coffee and playing a little poker.

The elders watched young Katy, now a sturdy nine-year-old, hitch up her rough pants, and stomp across the yard to the barn, one long pigtail bouncing beneath her Western hat. Her cowboy boots kicked up dust on the dry hard ground as she disappeared.

"You're going to make her just like yourself," said Evans in a warning voice.

"How's that?" asked Lefty.

"Hard as a corncob and twice as tough."

Sheriff Langdon began to laugh and the other two men, startled at first, joined in.

"Say," said Langdon. "Be hospitable, Lefty. Pour me some of that coffee!"

"Yuck! It's bitter as my Ma's medicine!" said Evans. "You should have milked the cow yourself, Lefty, afore we got here. You knew we was coming."

"Couldn't stop you riding in if I wanted to," growled Lefty.

"Well, we got an interest in Katy too," said the older rancher. "Wasn't we there when you got her? We got to see you're raising her right."

"Lefty, you're raising her up a boy!" said Langdon.

"No! A Westerner who knows the value of work!" drawled the girl's uncle.

"You mean your little slave," commented Evans. "Why, it's shameful how you have that purty little thing fetch and haul for you, if..."

"That's the truth," said the sheriff. "Why…

"Deal the cards, lawman, before the sun sets, and we got to light the lamp and fight the skeeters," said Lefty.

"Tarnation!" exclaimed Evans taking a sip of coffee and slamming the cup down. "You'd think a man having company would have the cream ready for this vile brew."

"If you want it that bad," said Lefty. "Go help Katy."

"I think I will," said Evans rising from the table.

The sheriff and uncle watched the older rancher walk across the yard and disappear into the barn. The sun was lingering to the West and lay high over the mountains, as bright and as hot as any regular Colorado day. A warm wind blew, and it rustled the pinion and cedar trees that grew close and on either side of the cabin porch. The strong clean scent of cedar hung in the air.

"Hello, Katy," greeted the rancher as he entered the barn.

"Oh, hello, Uncle Evans," said Katy. "You come to watch me work?"

"I did, and to get some of that milk, and to talk to my favorite niece."

"The pail's there, along with a clean wet rag to clean Petunia's udders."

"How you doing today, Katy?"

"Fine, can't wait to go to town tomorrow," answered the little girl. "Lefty promised to buy me a new pony! It'll be my birthday next week."

"I know. I been meaning to ask what you think you might like from me. I had my eye on a purty pink dress."

"Aww, Uncle Evans! I don't want no dress! But

you could buy me a new sombrero or a big checkered neckerchief."

"That's all?"

"That's all I need. Except…"

"What?"

"Gus at the gun shop has the purtiest little .32 revolver. Calls it a hide-out gun. It's nickel-plated and fits right in the palm of my hand."

"Katy! A girl shouldn't be thinking of sombreros and pistols and…"

"Why not?"

She stopped forking the tainted straw and manure into the wheelbarrow and now leaned on the wooden shaft, tines in the stall's dirt floor. Staring at her adopted uncle, genuine surprise showed on her face. Evans laughed.

"Katy, if you don't watch it, Lefty will have you turned into the biggest tomboy in all of Pueblo County."

"And what's wrong with that?"

"Because I want to see a girl as purty as you grow up to be a gentle and refined young lady."

"What does re-fined mean?"

"It means you are of the gentler sex, and you won't act like a boy."

"When I grow up," said Katy proudly. "I may not be as big, but I'll be tough, and I'll outride, outshoot, and out rope any cowboy."

"Is that what you really want, Katy?"

"It sure is."

"Well," sighed Evans. "I reckon you got a good head

start. Now let me milk this durn cow. I got to have some of that good stuff for your uncle's coffee. It's as bitter as alkali and twice as strong."

"Lefty says he likes it with bite. And I guess I do too."

"You mean you drink that stuff?" asked Evans, surprise showing on his face.

"Every morning at the crack of dawn," replied Katy proudly.

Evans carried the milk back to the front porch and set it down. He took the dipper hanging near the water olla and poured some fresh milk into the coffee. Then he set the dipper and milk bucket aside. Sitting down, he took a big sip of the coffee.

"Now," said Rancher Evans. "That's better! Deal those cards, boys. I'm feeling lucky tonight."

* * *

Katy Bennett stood with rifle in hand, waiting her turn. She wore a split leather skirt, a light blue silk shirt, a large pale embroidered yellow bandanna around her neck, and plain brown high heeled boots. Her straw-colored hair blew in the wind, and the shining wave of it fell down to her shoulders. Around her neck, hung by a leather string, was a brown sombrero. Every man and boy, from eight to eighty, had his eye on this slim girl. Katy was eighteen, and her sun-tanned and freckled face reflected a girl who worked and played hard. She was a prime example of a Western cowgirl from head to toe. Many a woman in the crowd looked on with curious envy.

"Ladiesssss and Gen-tle-mennnnn! Next up, and very last…we have Katy Bennett of the Bennett Ranch, competing for the first prize of FIFTY DOLLARS!" shouted the man through a large round megaphone, held up by extended arms and hands, mouthpiece to the announcer's lips. "As most of you folks know, Katy has won the prize three years in a row. The question is…can she do it again?"

Katy, standing erect, stepped forward. A hundred yards away across a large open field of beige ground and yellow grass stood a paper target with large round circles and in the middle a round black dot. It was nailed to a square board mounted on a tall post. Katy raised the rifle and brought it tightly to her right shoulder. All eyes of the crowd were on the young woman, who stood in perfect form. She aimed and squeezed the trigger, and the rifle blasted. Smoke billowed. Katy lowered the Winchester and ratcheted another shell into the chamber. She raised the rifle and fired again, and then a third time.

A horseman galloped for the target, the crowd murmured in eager anticipation.

"A woman ain't got no right in this here competition!" shouted some young wit, obviously under the influence.

"Who said that!" shouted Lefty.

"Behave yourself," exclaimed Rancher Evans to his friend.

"We should know pretty quick now," said Sheriff Langdon, standing close behind Katy.

The rider on the horse, dismounted at the target,

carefully tore the paper free and holding it one-handed, mounted and spurred his horse to a gallop and towards the crowd. Coming to a skidding halt, the rider dismounted, ran with target in hand, and gave it to one of three standing judges. They eagerly held it up and examined it. The men conferred, and then the announcer raised his megaphone again.

"Ladiessss and Gen-tle-mennnn, we have a winner! For the fourth time in a row, Katy Bennett wins the Pueblo County Fair's shooting contest and is the grand prize winner of FIFTY DOLLARS!"

The large crowd of spectators responded in a roar of clapping and enthusiastic shouting. A few young wags booed.

The three judges and the announcer went to Katy, who stood before the crowd. One of the men gave Katy a blue ribbon and another a large white envelope containing the prize money. The crowd continued to applaud and shout. This was the culmination of the County Fair's activities, and the people began to disperse. Katy found herself surrounded by her three uncles.

"Well, missy, I see you didn't take my advice," whispered Evans in the handsome girl's ear.

"I'm sorry," said Katy, "I can't hear you."

Evans repeated the response two more times and the third, loud enough for Lefty and the sheriff to hear.

"What advice?" shouted Lefty.

"That was meant for Katy's ears alone," said Evans.

"Did he tell you to miss?" asked Lefty angrily.

Katy smiled demurely, still holding rifle in one hand,

the blue ribbon and the prize money envelope in the other.

"How do you expect her to find a young man if she keeps scaring them off?" exclaimed Rancher Evans.

The sheriff laughed, and so did Katy.

"She's only eighteen!" shouted Lefty. "You want to go marrying her off when she's still a child?"

"Plenty of girls get hitched afore then!" shouted Evans back at Lefty.

"Suppose," said Sheriff Landon, "we all head for the ranch before we continue this conversation."

"Not yet," said Katy."Gus has the prettiest little six-shooter, and I had him put it aside just in case I won. If you want to stay with me, I'm stopping there first."

"Katy!" said Evans. "You shouldn't spend that money, but put it aside for a rainy day."

"If she won it," exclaimed Lefty in a loud voice. "She can spend it as she pleases."

"I'm just trying to…" began Evans.

"Wait until we get Katy home before blabbin' personal business," interrupted the sheriff.

The three men, still arguing heatedly, followed Katy off the field and to their horses. From there, the four rode from the fairgrounds to the gun shop in town. The young woman got her new pistol, and they mounted and rode to the Bennett ranch. The heated discussion between the three men continued unabated while the girl rode silently along. From time to time, a smile or frown came to her face when one of the men said something particularly amusing or onerous.

* * *

Sheriff Langdon and Rancher Evans met Lefty and Katy on the street in front of the large one-room schoolhouse. Each of them was dressed in Sunday best, and Katy wore her usual Western wear, refusing to match the other girls' evening finery. In most men's opinion, both young and old, this made her all the more attractive. Her long hair, under a Western hat, gave the lovely curve of her face a boyish charm. She was darkly tanned and wore no makeup.

Due to the hard work of riding, roping, branding, mending fences, cutting and stacking hay, and various duties about the ranch, Katy was whip-cord strong. She came prepared for dancing, still dressed in her split-leather skirt, silk blouse, and vest. She changed her boots for Apache Moccasins, a gift from a Jicarilla Apache. A Saturday night social was more endurance than dancing. A girl had to be strong to keep up with the young males and their energetic stomping.

"Katy," said Rancher Evans. "I see you're not wearing the dress I sent you. Mrs. Carlisle said it would fit you. Was there something wrong…"

"It fit fine, Uncle," responded Katy. "But it just wasn't to my taste. I put it back in the box just as you sent it."

"But Katy, I was told it was of the latest fashion, and to me it…"

"Can't you see my niece don't go for all that fancy nonsense," exclaimed Lefty.

"I was just trying…"

"To marry off our niece again," laughed Sheriff Langdon.

"Exactly," said Lefty.

"Well, she is turning twenty-two, and…" began Evans.

"If the three of you are going to rehash marriage and my age in front of me yet again, and as if I'm not even present, I'm going to scream," said Katy. "Uncle Evans, I appreciate what you have been trying to do for me all these years, but I am the daughter of Kenny Bennett and the niece of Lefty, and on our ranch, we don't put on airs. A man will have to accept me as I am and to tell you the truth, I haven't found one to my suiting. Until I do, I will no longer take kindly to your interference."

It was a long speech for Katy, and the uncles were taken by surprise. So much so that they stopped talking, paused on the dirt street, all three with quizzical expressions on their faces and mouths open.

"Don't look so surprised," said Katy. "I got a mind of my own, and from now on, I'm going to use it."

"That's speaking your piece!" exclaimed Lefty, beaming proudly.

Katy walked hurriedly before the three men and disappeared into the crowded doorway of the schoolhouse. The uncles followed, in time to see a line of eligible young Westerners rush to ask Katy for a dance. Already the musicians were lined up on a wooden platform at the back of the room, men in shirt sleeves and garters, a voluntary group who took their music-making seriously. Completing the lineup tonight were two violinists, a banjo player, a guitarist, and one old fellow on a piano. They were enthusiastically playing their instruments, if not harmoniously and on key, at least with a unified pulsing rhythm. Katy was swept up in the arms of one cowboy and, within seconds, was on the crowded dance floor swirling in a large circle.

More than any other girl, Katy put in hours of uninterrupted dancing. She swirled around the hardwood floor with every young and eligible man in the place. Unlike other girls her age, she did no flirting; she gave no young fellow coy looks or pretended to be too tired to dance with boys and men of lesser attraction. Katy was a favorite precisely because she danced with any man who asked her. At least once.

Eventually, even Katy needed a break. Seeking cool air and a drink, she left the throng of men behind, pleading a needed rest. The girl went outside to the lemonade stand and unpretentiously grabbed a glass and gulped down the entire contents. Then she set it aside and picked up another.

"I see that you're enjoying yourself," said an unfamiliar voice.

There was something about the tone and tenor that struck the young women's interest. The deep timbre of it vibrated melodiously. Katy turned and saw standing before her a very handsome fellow. He was at least one head taller than she, had broad shoulders, and wore a suit of eastern fashion. Upon his head was some short-brimmed chapeau no Western man would ever think of wearing. The stranger smiled. Katy was smitten the instant she had turned to see the face that matched the voice.

"I…," began Katy and then stopped.

For the first time in her life, she was flustered, and it took a few seconds to gain composure.

"Excuse me," she began again. "You took me by surprise. You said something to me?"

To her own chagrin, Katy found herself flirting with a man. So this is what it's like, she thought to herself.

"I said," began the stranger, "that I see you are enjoying yourself."

"Oh yes!" flashed Katy with her most ingratiating smile. "I always do."

"First thing I thought when I set eyes upon you," said the tall young man, "was, now there is a girl who doesn't put on airs."

"Haven't thought about it," replied Katy.

"I know I'm right," said the stranger, and he laughed. "Let me introduce myself. I'm Tom Sherwood."

"Oh! Like Sherwood Forest in the tales of Robin Hood! I loved those stories."

"Me too. I'm sorry, I'm at a disadvantage..."

"Pardon me?"

"Your name, I didn't…"

"It's Katy! Katy Bennett."

Tom put out his large hand. The young woman stepped forward and shook it, her grip as strong as any man.

"Firm handshake," smiled Tom. "Tell me, do you do everything as energetically as you dance?"

Katy looked up and thought seriously on the question.

"Yes! Now that you mention it, I do."

"And you don't believe in holding back? Not even just a little bit?"

"Why should I? If I know I'm good at it?"

Tom Sherwood laughed again. At first, Katy gave

him a startled and annoyed look, then succumbed to his jocularity and joined in.

"What are we laughing about?" asked Katy.

"I must say you are a refreshing change from any woman I have ever met. You wouldn't by any chance be married or engaged…"

"Heavens, no!"

"Good! If I may, would you like to dance with me? Maybe afterward, talk?"

Katy took a large sip from the lemonade she held in her hand and then discarded the rest of the liquid onto the ground in a quick snap of the wrist. She set the glass back on the table. During the exchange, the young woman had found that she had blocked out the crowd's noise and the music. A bit dizzy, she put a hand to a flushed forehead, regained her wits, and looked around. There were countless unfriendly stares from young men standing in front of the school. She turned and flashed a smile at the interesting stranger.

"Tom, you know there are others waiting to dance with me?"

Again the tall man tilted back his head and laughed.

"Katy, I'm positive you will have no trouble making up your mind. The invitation stands."

She reached out and gave Tom Sherwood her hand. Both smiling, the couple entered the schoolhouse. They had to push their way through unfriendly bystanders. Taking her in his arms, Tom began to lead Katy around the dance floor. And, as she expected, the man held and glided her effortlessly around the circle. They moved in perfect rhythm to the music, and every eye in the room was upon the stranger and the young woman.

People pointed and talked. A buzz went through the crowd. Who was this fellow?

The talk expanded when abruptly, at the end of the dance, the strangely dressed Easterner took Katy's hand and led her toward the door. Angry Westerners accosted the couple, trying to keep them from leaving the building. Struggling, Tom and Katy made it outside. Men followed, and Micky Laycock, the son of the saloon keeper, Baldy Laycock, yelled out.

"How come you came to our town and molest our women?"

Many from the schoolhouse flooded outside to hear and see the confrontation. Micky was clearly enjoying the sudden attention. Other young men added voices of complaint. Feeling confident, Micky continued.

"You come into our town in your fancy clothes and think you can just take the first purty girl that comes along?"

Murmuring comments assented in multiple expressions of anger.

"Stop that!" said Katy in a voice loud enough for the crowd to hear. "What I do is MY business."

The crowd gasped and fell silent. Momentarily set back, Micky frowned and then laughed, gathering his wits.

"Afraid to let the greenhorn speak for you, Katy?"

The crowd jostled closer, and voices murmured.

"No, I'm not afraid to speak for myself," said Tom Sherwood in his deep bass voice. "Is this the Western hospitality I heard so much about?"

"We don't let strangers come into town and take our women!"

"And I don't let bullies push me around," replied the easterner.

Tom Sherwood pushed bodies aside and walked forward. Micky stood, feet spread wide apart, in the middle of the street. When Tom came near the loudmouthed bully, he stopped. In a quick movement, Micky threw a right-hand punch. The stranger ducked and then drove a fist into Laycock's face. The crowd rushed forward, not to miss any of the action. They groaned in disappointment when Micky fell flat on his back, out cold.

"Anyone else?" asked Tom Sherwood, standing before the prone man.

"What is this?" demanded Baldy Laycock, coming through the crowd.

Sheriff Langdon appeared from nowhere.

"Nothing for you to be concerned about, Baldy," said Langdon. "Your boy over-stepped himself."

"What did he do?" asked Baldy.

"He loudmouthed this stranger and my niece. The big fellow defended her," answered the lawman.

The crowd began to disperse and then stopped to listen to what may become a more serious dispute.

"Look out!" said Katy.

Micky Laycock had come to. He pulled a revolver and

was aiming it at the back of the Easterner. From a pocket in her vest, Katy held a hide-out gun and fired. The little .32 caliber bullet pierced the wrist of the prone troublemaker, and his pistol dropped.

Baldy Laycock roared loudly in alarm and thrust himself forward through the crowd.

"How many times have I told you to keep that iron in your holster!" shouted Baldy at his son.

The angry father grabbed Micky and hauled him to his feet.

"It hurts," complained the son.

"Keep being stupid, and I'll really give you something to complain about. You darn fool, you let a girl shoot you!"

"That's no girl," exclaimed the wounded young man. "That's Katy Bennett."

"Serves you right. How many times have I told you to leave the Bennetts alone. Come on, we need to find the doc."

The crowd separated, and the two Laycocks hurried up the street.

"Thanks," said Tom Sherwood, turning to see Katy drop the little pistol into her vest pocket.

"Suppose you two call it a night," suggested the sheriff.

Behind them, Evans and Lefty came forward.

"Are you all right, Katy?" said Evans.

"You have to ask that after what she just done?" beamed Lefty.

"Come on," said Sheriff Langdon. "Let's get our horses and see Katy home."

"Tom," said the girl. "If you'd like to visit tomorrow, you'd be welcome. We're at the Bennett Ranch. You just ask, and folks will tell you where."

In the dispersing crowd, Tom Sherwood watched Katy, and her three uncles walk up the street. Attempting to avoid further attention, the big man headed for the hotel and his room.

* * *

Baldy Laycock, a bully, was a brute of a man, nearly six feet tall. Now he was more enraged than when his brother was killed by Kenny Bennett. At that time he could do nothing. But now that his son Micky had been publicly humiliated, the Bennett's must be repaid. Baldy's plan was simple and direct. His men would wait for that stranger, and when he left his hotel, he would be ambushed. There would be retribution.

* * *

Late into the night, Tom Sherwood paced, tossed, and turned. Alternately he arose from his bed, lit, and blew out the lamp. Several times he tried to read a story from a book by Mark Twain and got lost in the words. His fevered mind was haunted by the vision of that girl. Never had he met a woman of such beauty and strength. But she was obviously much more than that. Katy was full of life and energy, a person wholly to herself. She was unique and as tough as nails. Hadn't she proven that last night when she saved his life?

And who are those three men who looked after her?

He wondered. First the sheriff, and then the two tough-looking Westerners who came to escort her away. No doubt family. They didn't seem to bat an eye when she shot that hoodlum, and they didn't even arrest the pistol-toting brute.

Tom was no stranger to violence or killing. But one didn't expect such a thing on the open streets of a town. If that was the way it was going to be, he would wear his pistol from now on. That shoulder holster he had purchased would go well with his .36 army revolver. It would fit nicely hidden under his jacket. It was the very same pistol he carried with the 18th Ohio Infantry. He knew what violence of any kind could lead to.

First thing in the morning, he would wash and put on clean clothes, take breakfast, and then find a horse at the stable. Katy had said all he had to do was ask. From what he had seen last night, no doubt everyone knew the Bennetts.

* * *

Tom Sherwood arose early, heart pumping with adrenaline and anticipation. *Now that I met the most charming young woman on earth, I better not mess this up.*

Breakfast was an ample affair, followed by several cups of dark hot coffee. It was a fitting beginning to the momentous day.

Tom burst from the wide hotel entrance onto the large porch. Bright rays of the Western sun pierced his eyes and made him squint. A pale blue sky spread out in a wide dome above the buildings of the town. It was like any other day in the sunny West, but to Tom, it felt special. A smile flashed across his face, and he hurriedly went down the steps and crossed the dirt street towards the livery.

Baldy Laycock sent for three of his best men, Al, Harry, and Breezy.

"Hide, and when you confront him, wear bandannas," growled Baldy. "Knock the stranger senseless, then beat him with clubs. Smash in his face, break every bone in his body, and pound him to an inch of his life. Don't mess this up."

Baldy was in a rage for vengeance. His anger relayed fear in his men, and they vowed to follow through.

Al was Baldy's most trusted man. When he saw the stranger walk towards the stable, they ran through alleys and the back part of town and entered the building through the rear. The hostler was an old man, and Al himself tapped his skull. Then they tied and gagged the old fellow and set him in his living quarters. They were none too soon. The Easterner came to the wide front door of the stable and called out.

"Hello? I'd like to rent a horse."

Silence greeted Tom, and he entered into the darker confines. Perhaps the stable owner was in the back or by the corrals. Tom kept calling out, and a sixth sense, one that had served him well in the war, warned him of danger. When a dark shadow behind him appeared, he dodged. The club intended for the back of his head struck his shoulder a glancing blow and knocked him sideways. In an instant, Sherwood had his colt in hand and turned and clubbed down with pistol barrel. It was a solid blow, and the fellow collapsed.

From behind a pile of hay appeared two more men, bandannas covering their faces. Each held a club, and they were rushing forward.

"Stop, or I'll shoot!" shouted Tom.

One man hesitated, and the other kept coming. Tom fired, aiming for the right shoulder. The pistol blasted loudly, and the fellow was struck. He dropped his club and fell forward onto the dirt floor. Stepping back, Tom held his revolver at the ready. The last man standing turned and ran out the back door. The thug he struck remained prone on the ground, out cold. The wounded man writhed in pain, holding a right hand to a bloody shoulder.

It wasn't long, and Tom heard running footsteps. Several men came near the stable.

"What's going on?" asked one of the men standing out of sight in the street.

"Get the sheriff!" shouted Tom.

Men's voices were heard, but no man was foolish enough to enter.

"This is Sheriff Langdon! What's going on?"

"It's all right, sheriff," called Sherwood. "Three men tried to attack me. I shot one and knocked out another. The third man ran away."

Langdon entered, pistol in hand. He assessed the situation.

"Some of you out there," ordered the sheriff, "come open that door in the back and let in some light."

Two from the growing crowd outside entered the stable and complied with the lawman's instructions. The sheriff bent down and rolled over the man who lay unconscious and pulled the bandana down.

"Why, it's Al Mosley," said the sheriff. "And the wounded man is Breezy."

"I got to have a doc," moaned Breezy, holding a dirty handkerchief to a shoulder wound.

"One of you men go get Doc Campbell," called out the lawman.

Eventually, the doctor came, and under his orders, both men were carried to his office and laid out in the back room. The sheriff dispersed the other men, all except Tom Sherwood.

"I'll remove the bullet from Breezy, and he'll be just fine," said the doc, "if poison and fever don't set in. But Al got his skull crushed, and I'm not sure he's going to make it."

"Thanks," said the sheriff. "I'll get a man to stand watch over these two until you say they can be moved to the jail. Now," said the sheriff to Tom, "suppose we go to my office for a talk."

At the jail, the sheriff sent a deputy to the doc's office. Tom Sherwood had remained reticent the entire time.

"You're a man of few words," said Langdon.

"Would it have done any good to say more?" asked Sherwood.

The sheriff eyed the big fellow. He noted the black suit he wore and the funny little hat. There was something strong and substantial about the Easterner.

"Show me where you keep it," said the sheriff.

Tom held back his suit jacket and exposed a shoulder holster.

"You always carry it that way?"

"No. I bought this rig when I knew I was coming west. Put it on after the trouble last night."

"Expecting more, were you?" asked Langdon.

"No, but I wanted to be able to defend myself."

"You've used that Colt before," said the sheriff.

"I have. Carried it in the war."

"Where?"

"The Ohio 18th…fought at Stone River and Chickamauga."

"I see. You handled yourself pretty well in that stable. Up until today, Baldy Laycock and his men have gotten away with every shady deal they've tried. Thanks to you, if I can get one of those two men to talk, I'll be arresting Baldy. He'll either pull freight, or we'll have to shoot it out. He's not a man to be arrested easily."

"I had my share of fighting," said Tom. "I hope you don't ask me for help."

"Not even if I told you it would protect Katy Bennett?"

"That's different. In that case, I'll do whatever you ask."

"Your name's Tom Sherwood?" asked the lawman.

"It is."

"Well," said the sheriff, suddenly smiling and putting out his right hand. "Welcome to Pueblo. If I figure right, I think my niece Katy has just found herself a right good man."

Tom looked up and studied the lawman's face. Then he put out a hand, and both men shook.

"You on your way to visit Katy?" asked the now friendly sheriff.

"I was. Soon as I can find a horse and directions."

The lawman laughed. Taking a wanted poster and a pencil lying on his desk, he turned the paper over and quickly drew a map.

"Take the buckskin tied to the railing out front," said the sheriff opening the door. "That's my horse—his name's Burt. I'd be right proud if you ride him out to see Katy. Take my advice, son. Be direct. Get her away from Lefty. Take a ride or a long walk, and then tell her how you feel. You're the first man I ever saw Katy side up with. If I got it right, she'll say yes."

Sheriff Langdon stood on the boardwalk in front of his office and watched the wide back of the stranger as he rode down the street. Unknown to him, passersby stared at the broad and unfamiliar smile on the lawman's face.

A CHRISTMAS STORM

It was one day before Christmas, and a storm from the north was brewing. A strong cold wind began to blow across the open prairie. The temperature dropped; spits of snow began slowly, then in earnest, falling heavily, unendingly, coating the land with frozen white. It was a savage storm, as if some evil force or Satan himself spurred it on.

Several fragile parties traveled across the Great Plains before the Wet Mountains of Colorado. Their human struggle to stay alive played out before the eyes of two powerful forces, from Heaven and Hell. Some would call it fate, but a believer would recognize the influence of the two realms in the never-ending conflict for the soul of humanity.

* * *

A year before, Big Bear had led his wife, Gray Feather, down the trail. Following behind came his wife's sister, Little Deer, and beside her walked the warrior's six-year-old son Black Tail. They had struggled east over the mountains and toward the Front Range of Colorado.

The Bear family was escaping the soldier attack on the White River Agency. They were away gathering fuel when the soldiers' assault began. The family, lucky to survive, ran for their lives, seeking a safe refuge.

* * *

At the endless sounds of gunshots, Big Bear told his family he must go back.

"No, don't," pleaded Gray Feather. "There are too many soldiers. Stay and protect your family."

"I am a warrior, woman. I must go."

"And if you die, what happens to us?"

Big Bear loved his family. He looked on the faces of his son, wife, and her sister. He hesitated. Shouting and repeated gunshots echoed in the distance. His warrior spirit called him to do battle and fight for the tribe. Big Bear turned and ran toward the sound of conflict. As he rounded the trail, he saw nearly two hundred soldiers below. The small Ute band, led by Chief Captain Jack, was attacking the soldiers. Joining the battle from above, Big Bear began to shoot arrows at the blue coats. Then he saw Captain Jack kill Major Thornburgh. More than a third of the soldiers lay dead or wounded.

Big Bear climbed down and went to Captain Jack's side. It was from him he learned that the vile Indian Agent, Meeker, and his followers were dead. Briefly, the Ute fighters rejoiced. They had defeated and pinned down a superior number. Those soldiers still alive were hiding behind their dead horses.

Despite worry over his family, Big Bear followed his

leader's orders. For two days, they fought against the enemy. Then came the Buffalo Soldiers from Fort Lewis. They attacked and pushed away the Indian ambush. Big Bear, Captain Jack, and the Utes continued to resist, even when their ammunition was gone. Then a Ute warrior came with a message that four hundred fifty more soldiers were on their way. Knowing they were defeated, Big Bear took a parfleche of food and supplies and escaped to the south. Never again would he and his family live on a cruel reservation.

As the warrior came down off high ground, several soldiers rose before him and began shooting. An arrow at the ready, it was released, and Big Bear watched it pierce the coat of a uniform, and then he ran. One time he stumbled, heard weapons discharge, and still he fled, feeling the white-hot heat of a bullet in his side.

Coming to a turn in the trail, Big Bear slowed and looked back. There were only two uniformed soldiers from Fort Lewis, one man white and the other black. The warrior dare not lead these two enemies to his family. Instead, he turned, nocked an arrow, and swiftly released it. The shaft hit the thigh of the white, the soldier fell with a scream and dropped his rifle. Big Bear ran forward, nocking another arrow. Before the Buffalo Soldier could fire his weapon, Gray Feather and Little Dear came from cover. They beat the Buffalo Soldier back with sticks of wood. The black man dropped his rifle and Big Bear ran forward, his arrow still at the ready.

By the time he came close, the two Indian women had picked up the fallen rifles and pointed them at the soldiers.

The black private held up his arms in surrender.

"You, I no kill," said Big Bear. "But the white…"

"No!" commanded Gray Feather. "We go now before it is too late."

Big Bear stared down at the white man in a grimace of hate and then back at the other soldier.

"Why do you come?" asked Big Bear to the black man. "Why do you fight for such as these?"

The private held his arms high, and sweat appeared on his forehead. He lowered a hand to wipe it away, and his cap fell from his head. Big Bear stared at his curly hair in wonder and then repeated his question.

"Why?"

"Being a soldier is better than laboring in the fields," responded the prisoner. "I don't ask why. I just follow orders."

"Come!" said Gray Feather looking down at the dripping crimson from the wound in her husband's side. "You are hurt. We must go…"

There was shouting from other soldiers coming up the trail, then gunfire. Big Bear glared with fierce hatred. Feeling the pain in his side, he touched the wound with his right hand and then held it up before him. It was bright red.

"You do wrong to fight for these..." said Big Bear looking at the Buffalo Soldier and then pointing with his bow at the wounded white man.

"I have no choice," replied the black soldier.

"I give you choice. I give you life!" shouted Black Bear, hotly spitting out the words. "Go, and fight my people no more!"

Then the warrior allowed his wife to pull him off the trail into the brush.

* * *

Traveling for over a year, climbing and descending mountains, taking game trails, facing cold weather and starvation, Big Bear's family was exhausted. The four from the Northern Ute Band, man, wife, sister, and child, barely survived. They would never see their people again. They would rather die than return to the reservation.

Often they hid or traveled by night, escaping the fear and wrath of white settlers. It was in late December that they came down out of the mountains and onto the grasslands. For a time, it was warmer, and they were sheltered by the Front Range of mountains from the fierce winds. Their supplies were meager and they had suffered the entire trip. Only the hunting skills of Big Bear kept his small family alive.

The warrior survived the gunshot, but the bullet remained. The flesh in his side only partly healed over. Now, after all this time, it was beginning to fester, and the Ute Warrior started to weaken. Knowing his family relied on him, he was afraid to tell them he was failing. Worse, his wife was swollen with child. Big Bear knew not what more he could do but travel south into a warmer climate. Then, down on the prairie, the temperature dropped, and walking south, the four Indians fought to stay alive in a growing blizzard.

* * *

A stagecoach headed south, its next destination Trinidad, Colorado. Horses hit a low spot in the rough dirt road. The trail was flooded, and the team struggled through it, pulling hard. The driver tensed and jerked on reins, too late. Two wheels on the ride side of the coach dug deep and then sank in the mud. The horses were jerked back, the tongue broke, and the heavy vehicle fell viciously, as the stage tumbled on its right side.

The driver, reins wrapped around his wrist, was pulled high into the air and came down on the kicking horses tangled up in singletrees and yokes. Several kicks from a large hoof of a stricken horse broke the driver's neck and crushed his head. Inside the coach, a mother, a young girl, and the baby were thrown heavily to the right. The older woman hit her head on the door frame and was instantly killed. The young girl and baby were saved by the body of their mother. The guard on top, throwing down his shotgun, jumped as the wagon fell and landed safely in the soft mud.

Three horses continued kicking and screaming. One had a broken tongue stuck deep in its belly. Two other horses had broken legs, and the fourth was able to stand. The guard came around to look at the team and, annoyed by the screaming horses, pulled his pistol and shot three of the injured animals in the head. The last of the gunshots echoed off into the distance. A cold wind blew harder, and the guard tried his best to scrape mud from his clothing.

"Mister!" cried Sally, the young girl holding the baby. "Mister! Will you help me? My mother is hurt."

Reluctantly, the stagecoach guard circled around the

water and mud and to the rear of the coach. The man climbed up the boot and looked through the door window.

"Please help us?" begged Sally looking into the guard's eyes.

"Here, reach the baby up, and I'll take her."

Sally did as she was told. The man carefully laid the bundle on the stagecoach side. Then, reaching in, grabbed the girl's outstretched arms and pulled her through the opening. Then the guard helped the girl down the boot. He picked up the baby and carefully climbed down. He handed the infant to Sally.

"My mother, mister, can you help her?"

Sighing, the guard went back up and opened the door. He managed to lower himself inside. It wasn't difficult to see the woman was dead. She had a broken neck. The wind outside was howling now, and the temperature was dropping. As an afterthought, the guard removed a heavy coat from the dead woman. Standing, he placed it outside, climbed up and out. Sliding down off the boot, he tossed the coat to the girl. He watched as she began to cry.

"Mama?"

"Little lady," said the guard, "she's gone."

The man walked around the back of the coach, and lying in the mud, were suitcases and two chests. The guard pulled one heavy chest out of the mud and then the other.

"Here, you sit down," said the guard. "I have to see to the horse."

Sally pulled her mother's coat around her and the baby and then sat on one of the chests. The heavy coattails shielded her bottom from the cold metal. The wind blew harder and howled as it crossed the open plains. The overturned coach blocked some of its strength. The girl held her infant sister closer. Unfolding a part of the blanket wrapped around the baby, Sally looked at her sister's face and saw her fast asleep. Folding the blanket again, the girl shuddered from the cold wind and pulled the thick collar around her head with her free hand.

The guard came back with the single large draft horse. Tying a makeshift rein to the coach's heavy rear wheel, the guard pulled the other heavy chest towards him. Taking out his pistol, he reloaded the three spent shells, then aimed and shot the lock off the chest. Pulling several gold sacks out, the guard put them in a canvass bag he carried over one shoulder. Sally watched. The baby didn't cry at the heavy explosion of the pistol, but the girl jumped.

"Are we going now?" asked Sally. "What do we do about the driver and my mother?"

"I'm afraid I couldn't carry you and the baby. It's only a little way to Trinidad," lied the guard.

As the man spoke, he untied the horse. The draft animal was large, so he climbed up on the boot of the wagon, the heavy canvass bag in one hand and the reins in the other. Then the man slid one leg over the horse and mounted. As an afterthought, he reached up inside the coach's boot and pulled out a wool blanket. This he tossed on the ground next to Sally.

"You wait here, little lady. I'll be back with help."

Sally watched the man's behavior, and not once did he look at her. The guard thumped heels in the animal's sides, and the horse moved forward, around the water and mud and back onto the rough road. It wasn't long, and both disappeared.

* * *

Coming across the prairie in the building storm were two wagons, their gray canopies snapping wickedly in the blowing snow and wind. Huddled under thick buffalo robes, two black families endured the cold. Worn-out mules, four to each wagon, pulled as best they could through the storm. It was so cold, the flakes came down dry and powdery. So far, the wind had blown the trail mostly clear, but as time sped by, they encountered deeper drifts that made the mules pull hard in their traces.

The family, traveling west, sought freedom, and against all hope, a place far away from hatred. They were a group of former slaves that still bore the names given to them by their past masters. Driving the first wagon was Benjamin Franklin Moses, and beside him in the wagon was his wife, Petunia. In the wagon bed, encroached in blankets and more buffalo robes, was the matriarchal leader, Ma Moses. Benny's son, George Washington Moses, drove the second wagon. In the back, also bundled up from the freezing cold, was his wife, Winnie, and their six-year-old son, Jessie.

"We best find shelter, or we're gonna freeze," called Ma Moses.

"Farmer Carter said there weren't no storms such as these this far south," Benny shouted back to his mother.

"Didn't I tell you, you can't trust no white man and lies he tells," yelled Petunia from the driver's seat.

"Ma," called Benny. "Ever since they killed Little Frank back in St. Louis, we've had nothin' but bad luck."

"Luck is what you make it," declared Ma Moses. "We've been struggling and fighting since our people's been brought here. We'll keep on and make our own peace. God gives us challenges, and so long as we're breathing, if we stay together, we'll find a way."

"But Ma," responded Benny. "The storm's getting worse."

"Makes no never mind. You got to get these animals out of this fierce wind. This is a regular blizzard that shows no signs of stopping. The animals may very well freeze to death."

"Not to say nothin' bout us!" shouted Petunia back to her mother-in-law.

"I see off the trail up yonder a group of boulders against the mountain," shouted Benny. "And, further on, plenty of trees for firewood."

"If you think you can get the mules and wagons there, then do it before it's too late." called out Ma.

Following his elderly mother's encouragement, as Benny had all his life, the middle-aged man turned the wagon off the trail and headed west toward the boulders. The second wagon followed, moving toward the giant chunks of granite—rocks that had fallen off the mountain and rolled down among the low green forest of cedar and pinion pines.

Benny Moses had to use a whip on the mules' behinds to get them to pull and climb. He had an aversion to whips and with good reason, and it was the first time he had used it on the animals. But their lives were in the balance, and the man did what he had to do. Behind, he also heard the crack of a whip, as his son George followed his father's example. The two wagons finally drove through snow and into the shelter of two boulders as big as houses. At that moment, they encountered a fire and four living people sitting on logs before it.

"Lord in Heaven!" shouted Petunia. "Indians!"

It was the old woman who was first down off the back of the wagon, and without hesitation, still bundled in a rag blanket, she came up to the fire. It didn't take her a moment to identify a wounded man lying on a buffalo robe and beside him, a pregnant woman. And wrapped around them for warmth was a little Indian boy and another young Indian woman. It was evident they did not have enough coverings or supplies. If the storm persisted, it would not be long before they would freeze.

"Bless you!" called Ma Moses, raising her right hand. "We want no harm to come to youse or us."

For Big Bear, this was an embarrassment not to be tolerated. The bullet in his side had made him a weakling, and he knew he was dying. For the sake of his family, he swallowed his pride and answered the old gray-haired black lady.

"My woman," responded Big Bear. "She is ill from cold and big with child. My son and my woman's sister have no food. We share our fire if you help."

By the time Big Bear finished speaking, all the members

of the Moses family had surrounded Ma. They barely heard the weak response from the prone Indian. But it was enough for the old lady.

"Benny!" shouted Ma Moses. "You and George get the axes and start cutting firewood. Petunia, you get my medicine bag out of the wagon, and then gather the spare blankets and robes and cover these good folks. Jessie, you bring one of the food bags. Now hurry!"

From years of following her authority, no one in the Moses family defied the old woman's orders. Within moments each person acted. By the time Benny and George began hauling in great chunks of cut wood, Ma Moses had her medical kit out and was kneeling on a robe, examining the festered gunshot wound of Big Bear.

"The bullet has to come out," they all heard her tell the Indian.

"Too late," responded Big Bear. "I die. Help my family. They need food."

"Spoken just like a fool man," retorted Ma Moses. "I doctored from here to Athens, Georgia, and my fine Indian friend, I'm telling you when I take that bullet out and treat that wound, in a few weeks, youse be good as new."

Big Bear grunted unwillingly when the woman pushed on the infection. He looked down and saw the bulging wound and watched, fascinated, as the old lady continued prodding.

"And my woman?" asked Big Bear.

"She and the rest of your family will be just fine soon as they eat and get warm," replied Ma. "Looks to me like the young lady is expectin'. I'll take a look at her after I fix you up."

"You do this?" asked the wounded Indian. "Why?"

"Seems like you folks need our help," replied Ma Moses. "Appears like both our families' been pushed to this camp. Suppose we help each other? Maybe when youse better, you'll show us how to live in this country."

"You do good, we do good," promised Big Bear.

He said this and looked up and into the eyes of the old woman.

"Fine," said Ma Moses holding a big spoon with medicine on it. "Now swallow this laudanum. It'll make the pain less, then I'm gonna open that wound and fetch that bullet out."

* * *

Juan Garcia walked along a deer trail heading north, far from the town of Trinidad. He had been traveling for days, a fugitive from a knife fight with a white man who had killed his father. Together, Juan and his father, Jose, had worked in a Mexican saloon. They cleaned the place in the mornings, wiped out spittoons, swept floors, cleared away bottles, and did all kinds of odd jobs for the owner. Juan and his father would not get rich from such labor, but it provided a modest shelter in a shack behind the saloon, and food on the table.

The trouble began when a group of wild cowhands came into the saloon—gringo's who brought coin. Their bad manners and loud drunken voices were tolerated by the saloon owner. The fight started when his father, Jose, went to pick up a spilled spittoon. He began to wipe up the slippery brown contents that flowed onto the floor. When Jose bent over, a drunken cowhand applied his boot to the old man's rear, and the vicious, unwarranted kick sent him flying into the long bar. Jose struck his head on a wooden panel that broke, then fell prone and silent. Blood gushed from a wound on the scalp, and most of the cowhands in the saloon laughed uproariously.

Juan saw the entire incident from the open door at the back of the saloon and rushed to his father's side. In his hand, he carried a fairly clean towel, which he gently applied to the wound. Instantly the rag turned crimson. Trying to awaken his father, there was no response. He felt for a pulse and found none. His father was dead.

Without thinking, Juan rose from the floor. From his pocket, he took out the folding knife he used in his daily chores. The cowhand laughed and pointed at the small man who approached him. Anger and loss overwhelmed Juan. His father was dear to him and the only companion he had in this life.

Amongst the laughter of the many cowboys, Juan approached steadily, none seeing the small blade held in his hand against his side. It was only at the last minute did the eyes of the murderer turn from laughter to fear. Too late, the cowhand reached for his pistol just as Juan plunged the knife into the heart of the merciless stranger. This drunken white man killed his father for no other reason than sport.

Blood flowed from the cowboy's wound, as the man

fell and died. Laughter turned to rage as the cowboys witnessed their friend's sudden death. They advanced in anger, each man reaching for a pistol. Juan was little, but fast and agile on his feet. He bent down and took the killer's revolver. While running towards the back door of the saloon, Juan fired first and made the many drunken gringos duck for cover.

Out in the alley, Juan ran into the tiny shack he and his father called home. He took up several items of food and clothing and put them into beautifully carved saddlebags that lay upon their meager table. Jose had been teaching his son the trade. Their plan was that someday the two of them would open a leather and saddle shop together. Now that dream was lost forever.

Within minutes Juan ran through the alleys and back streets of Trinidad. Soon he was out upon the open prairie. Exposed, he hurried as fast as could toward the high mountain crags and canyons that bordered the northern part of this small and wild town. The cowboys sought their horses, and watching from a high peak, Juan observed them spread out as they frantically searched for him. Juan turned and walked north. After two days, he ran out of supplies. A man in this open country without a horse was as good as dead. How foolish that he did not take the killer's mount. What was horse theft compared to murder?

Wind howled from the north, and flakes of snow began to fall. Still, Juan Garcia trudged forward, his father's beautiful saddlebags resting comfortably across his back and chest.

In fact, they were the only things keeping him warm

in the growing blizzard. If he didn't find shelter soon, he would certainly freeze to death.

The young man grimaced.

It will not be hunger that will kill me, he thought. I did not stay to see my father buried. Will the saloon owner pay for the priest to say the words?

Coming up a hill, now covered in ever-deepening snow, Juan looked down onto a road that led north from Trinidad. Below was a stagecoach lying on its side. The humps of dead horses lay before the stage. A dead man lay upon one of the big animals. Juan carefully studied the scene through swirling snow. Next to the coach, Juan thought he saw movement. Eventually, he made out a young woman sitting on a box, a blanket spread about her, and in her arms, she held a bundle. In the manner she held it, it looked very much like a baby.

Curious, Juan remained and watched.

What is going on here? he wondered.

It was beginning to be difficult to see further as more snow kept swirling ever thicker in the growing blizzard. Taking one last look around, Juan searched the looming Wet Mountains to his left, and there he saw through swirling flakes, a jumble of giant boulders. Further on was a bright green forest of trees.

There would be the better shelter, thought Juan. If only I had an ax to cut firewood. But, I must first see about those people below.

Against his better judgment, Juan descended the hill and slowly came to the overturned stagecoach. Eventually, the female saw him and rose to her feet.

"Oh," said the young girl. "Are you the help the guard sent?"

"No," replied Juan. "What guard?"

Despite the cold, the young woman, clearly no older than twelve, began to cry. In her arms, the girl held a tightly wrapped bundle. Tears froze as they ran down her cheeks, and then a flow of words erupted from the child's mouth. Juan had to lean nearer to grasp their meaning in the blowing wind.

"God help us!" cried the girl. "We were traveling to Trinidad…Mama had a job there. A letter promised a room for clerking and cleaning. When the stagecoach turned over, Mama hit her head."

"She's still inside?" asked Juan.

"Yes," cried the girl. "Mama's dead, and the driver too. Three of the horses were shot by the guard. And then he took one and rode off saying he would return with help."

"The guard left you behind?" asked Juan incredulously in his soft Spanish accent.

"Yes!" replied the girl. "That was since early this morning, and he never…"

"But why did he leave you? And what have you in your arms?

The girl pulled back a covering, and Juan briefly saw the staring eyes of a little infant. Then she covered its head once more.

"I'm beginning to think he's a thief," explained the girl. "Look! The box I am sitting on is full of gold coins. That other box over there, the guard opened and took out several bags. I could tell by his eyes that he was going to steal it. He lied; he never sent anyone back to help us."

"I'm sorry, Miss, my name is Juan, and I have nothing for you. But this low ground is a bad place to stay. Already the stagecoach is much covered with snow. Let us leave here and go toward the mountains. I saw a place with better shelter."

"Thank you, Mister Juan. My name is Sally, and the baby's name is Ann. She's my little sister. And mister, what about Mama?"

"I am sorry, Sally," replied Juan. "We must go. Do you have anything you must take with you?"

"Some baggage, but how do we carry it? And mother... she is inside the coach."

"I am afraid," said Juan. "That we must look for ourselves and move quickly or freeze. Come, follow me."

They began to walk away, and then Juan had a sudden thought. If they were to survive afterward, how could they manage without money? Going to the open chest, he found several more bags of gold, and untying a string from around one, he saw twenty-dollar gold pieces. Tying it shut, he took all the sacks and stuffed them in his father's saddlebags. By now, his hands were nearly frozen and stiff from the numbing cold.

Going to the other chest, Juan tried to lift it. It was too heavy. The little man stared at it. With great effort, he managed to drag it some distance to a jumble of rocks. Working quickly, he kicked loosesnow and stones over the chest. Picking up the heavy saddlebag, they began walking up the hill toward the looming mountain. Sally, carrying her baby sister, followed.

Juan turned to the girl, but she said nothing.

"Mi amiga," said Juan, shivering fiercely from the cold. "If we, you and me, live through this, we will need money. All my life, I have been told it is wrong to steal. I am sure your mama said the same. When we have time… you and me…we will talk of this. But now, follow; we must hurry."

Together, Juan and the young lady, holding her baby sister, walked as rapidly as they could through the deepening snow. Each step was upward. The jumble of rocks was now hard to see.

* * *

During one part of the probing for the bullet, while biting down on a piece of leather, Big Bear grunted and passed out. Beads of sweat appeared on the man's forehead, then quickly turned to ice. The old black woman found and removed the bullet. With a cloth, she wiped the sweat crystals away. Applying her special poultice, Ma Moses covered and bandaged the wound with a clean cloth. During the procedure, without being asked, Little Deer quietly came forward and knelt beside the old lady. Deftly, she helped with bandaging.

Black Tail and Gray Feather stood near and watched. Big Bear's family bundled in the extra robes provided by Petunia.

Seeing their fear, Ma Moses explained.

"He needs rest and food. If there is no infection or fever, he will be fine."

Some or part of this must have been understood by the

Indians. Together they helped move Big Bear closer to the fire. Then they sat on a log near him. The roaring flames provided life-saving warmth.

"Ma," said Benny. "We's got plenty of firewood. And soon's we finished here, George and I can build some kind of tent up close to the fire."

"We can take the canvas covers from the wagons," shouted George over the roar of the wind. "But I'm afraid the mules are in poor shape."

"We got enough food to last several days," said Petunia. "But what then? If we share with these Indians, we won't…

"George and Benny can go hunting," interrupted Ma Moses. "If we have to, we'll eat one of the mules."

"Me help," said Little Dear, speaking for the first time.

"Good!" called Ma Moses over the wind, and then she pointed to Gray Feather. "Now, missy, come to the wagon. You and I need to talk about you and your baby."

Fear, combined with a hesitant trust, came over the face of the pregnant woman. Little Deer, giving encouragement, took her sister's hand and followed the old lady as she climbed up onto the wagon.

* * *

It was a whiteout, and Juan had never seen anything like it in his twenty-four years. Behind him followed Sally, still carrying the baby. It was strange that the infant did not cry. Worried that Sally would be lost in the snow, Juan had taken a length of leather string and tied it to her wrist and his own. Nearly at the end of their strength, they both began to stumble in the deepening drifts as they continued to fight the wind and cold.

Juan was not sure he was heading in the right direction. The boulders could not be seen, and everything about them was white. It was difficult to see even a few feet ahead. Still, the young man pushed forward, with his arm now protectively around the young girl holding the baby. Fear began to grow in his heart. And it was not just for him but for the two humans beside him. They climbed and repeatedly fell.

“Madre Dios!” exclaimed Juan.

Then once more, falling to their knees, he began to pray silently.

Holy Mother, please call upon the Lord to save this girl and this little baby. Forgive me for taking the life of that bad man who killed my father. Blessed Mother, please help me find shelter.

Dragging his nearly frozen body to his feet, Juan moved forward through the blinding snow. Using the last of his strength, still holding Sally and her baby tightly in his arms, they stumbled into a wall of rock. Hoping against hope, Juan now lifted and carried the exhausted girl and baby forward. He worked his way around the wall of granite and suddenly emerged into the confines of two huge boulders. Instantly there was less noise, wind, and snow. Before him, he saw a bright yellow flame and felt the warmth.

Thank you, blessed Mother Mary, thought the young man.

Then Juan, all his strength gone, cold beyond measure, stumbled and went to his knees, the girl and infant with him. And then he collapsed to the ground. Sally, still holding the baby, recovered her balance, and managed to sit up.

* * *

It was Christmas morning, and the blizzard had stopped. The sun was now shining through a bright azure sky, and there was not a cloud to be seen. Already the deep snow was melting, and the dry air sucked inches at a time away from drifts. Some melted into the ground that so badly needed moisture, but most of it just evaporated into the air. In two days, in this high desert, there would be no snow except in the dark shady areas, and even that would scarcely reveal the terrible storm that had raged over the gathering at the boulders.

Benny and George, with the help of Little Deer, followed a trail back into a hidden canyon that held a herd of mule deer. Two animals were shot and dragged back to camp. While the three were away, Ma Moses stood within calling distance as Gray Feather delivered her baby. She did it bravely and stoically, in the Indian way. Together, they came back to camp, Ma Moses carrying the baby. Gray Feather sat on a log near the fire and rested. Then, one at a time, two infants were placed in her arms to suckle, the new Indian baby and little Ann.

George, Benny, and Little Dear butchered the meat. Together they built up the fire and cooked the venison.

Juan and Sally had recovered from the cold and sat near the fire.

"The Lord works in most mysterious ways," said Juan.

"Indeed he does," agreed Ma Moses.

The strange gathering of people feasted around the campfire. Juan told his story first. Towards the end, he decided to hold back about the gold. He would wait and see how events unfolded. That morning, he found the leather saddlebags he dropped back on the trail. They were now hidden. He could search for the box of coins later.

As they sat around the campfire, time passed. The sun made its journey across the sky, and as it set, the temperature dropped thirty degrees. The fire was built up, and the people gathered coverings and blankets for warmth.

Benny, George, Petunia, Winnie, little Jessie, and Ma Moses sat together near the fire. Each contributed to their story. It was necessary to go as far back as Africa and tell of the slavers and slave ships. It took a long time, and everyone listened intently.

Sally came next. She told of her father's death and her mother's efforts to keep the family together. She explained the birth of her sister and cried as she quietly described how her mother died.

Big Bear was the least trusting, and it showed. Yet, with Gray Feather and Little Deer's help, in simple English, he hesitantly revealed their struggle to survive.

When their histories were concluded, no one said much of anything. Above, an unusually bright star shone down upon them, and their eyes studied the heavens in hushed silence. George got up and placed another log on the fire.

The only sound was the slight rustle of the night wind, the cracking of burning wood, and far away, the call of coyotes hunting in the night.

Finally, Juan broke the silence.

"Yesterday, when the storm was at its worst, I prayed," explained Juan. "My prayer was answered. I believe the Holy Father brought us together."

"And, I prayed," said Sally.

"Yes," said Ma Moses, "I believe we all asked the Good Lord for help."

The white-haired leader of her clan studied her family's faces. She then looked at Big Bear and his family: Gray Feather, Little Dear, Black Tail—then at Sally and Juan. The group around the blazing fire stared back at the old black woman and nodded their heads.

"The Devil," continued Ma Moses, "he tries his best to make us enemies, to make us fight, to struggle against one another. How strange that we come together on Christmas day. We've been given a gift. Let us be friends. Let us promise to help each other. Together, we have strength."

All through the evening, the fire burned, and its light held back the forces of darkness.

FOR THE LOVE OF A WOMAN

"I love you, you love me, and we love each other. Right?"

"Yes, of course. What's that all about? Go on with you, Al, get to your chores, I got mine to do. I've got the laundry and this afternoon some canning…"

"Well, Alice, there are more things in this life than work. I just wanted to tell you how I felt."

"It's five-thirty in the morning, Albert, and no time to be fooling…"

"Woman! Sometimes you just take the fun out of it all."

"Get out of bed, Al. I can hear the milk cow mooing."

"That's all we do around here, Alice. Work, work, work. One time I'd just like to stay in bed all day."

"You dream too much, Al. And a dreamer never gets anywhere. Now we're both going to get out of bed, and I'll have breakfast ready by the time you're back from the barn. That'll make you feel better."

"Sometimes, woman, a man needs a little more than bread and coffee; he needs…"

"Not in the morning, Albert! It's not decent!"

"No wonder we never had no children."

"Al! Don't you bring that up again! You want me to be nice to you, don't ever talk about that!"

"Well, I read in the paper about the orphan train coming through town. We could…"

"NO! I won't have no half-raised orphan from New York City come stealing and upsetting our lives. We're doing just fine."

"No, Alice, we aren't, and you know it."

"Albert, not another word, or you can go to Hades! Fix your own darn breakfast and see if I care,"

Alice pulled the sheet up to her eyes as she tried to hide the crying and sniffling.

"I'm sorry, Alice. I'm an old fool. I'll go milk the cow and take care of the sow and the hosses. You just forget I said anything."

"Too late to apologize now, Al, now that you got me all upset. Go on, old man, go do your work. I'll do mine."

There was complete silence as Al got up in the dark, found his shirt and trousers on the chair, and pulled them on. He sat lacing up his boots and tried to leave the bedroom quietly. In the open room of their little farmhouse, he tripped over the butter churn, and it fell with a terrific crash. Alice, her head tucked under the sheet, smiled inwardly to herself.

He is an old fool, she thought. *But I do love him, despite how riled he gets me. Maybe tonight I can be nicer. Take time to bake a good apple pie. I got those apples the neighbors brought, wouldn't take long to fix.*

Al went to the barn and lit the lantern. By single light, he milked the cow. The silly thing kept moving her hooves. The rancher pressed his forehead against her side while he reached for her teats. Lilly, the cow, sidestepped and pushed the man off the three-legged stool and onto his back. The bucket, a quarter full of milk, also tipped over and spilled on the ground.

"Lilly!" shouted Al angrily, getting to his feet.

He took the lantern, found a lead rope, tied it to Lilly's halter, and then to a ring on a post. Then he righted the stool and bucket, sat back down, and commenced to milk. The coarse warm hide of the cow felt comforting to the forehead of the middle-aged rancher. He continued automatically to perform the task at hand, deftly squeezing and listening to the hiss of the stream of milk as it hit the inside of the bucket.

I shouldn't have upset Alice like that, thought Al. *I guess sometimes I just talk before thinking it through. Just say the first thing that pops into my mind, like the darn dumb fool I am. I should make it up to her. There is that bolt of cloth I hid away for her birthday. I guess I could get it out of the hayloft and give it to her early. Then I could buy her another present this Saturday before her birthday comes. Yes! That'll make her feel better!*

Al slopped the hogs and pitched hay to his gelding mustang and to his two draft horses. Then he climbed the ladder to the loft, and back behind the hay was a little hidden cupboard he had built. He pulled it open. Wrapped in a flour sack was the bolt of cloth. He took sack and cloth and went outside. The sun was up, and in the early light of the day, he slipped the flour sack down and looked at the flowered print pattern of blue cloth.

She should like this, thought Al.

"Alice!" he shouted as he made his way into the house.

The main room smelled of fresh brewed coffee and ham and eggs. There was also the fragrance of toasted bread. Alice never failed to whip up a good breakfast.

"I'm right here, Al," she said, standing at the table and setting down the coffee pot on a trivet.

"Alice," said her husband, holding the gift behind his back. "Sometimes I just talk too much. Here, woman, I got you something."

"What?" said his wife, taking the proffered flour sack.

She held the gift in one hand, slid the chair out with the other, and sat down. On a clean bare spot on the table, she placed the oblong object. Then she reached inside and pulled the bolt from the sack.

"Al!" Alice exclaimed. "What a beautiful pattern!"

"I thought it would make a mighty fine Sunday-go-to-meeting dress, Alice."

"Oh, yes! But how? You haven't been to town in two weeks. Did you have this hidden away? My birthday…"

"Your birthday doesn't have anything to do with it!" lied Al. "Can't a man buy his wife a gift any time he feels like it?"

"Al," said Alice. "How sweet! You haven't done anything like this since our first year of marriage."

"Well, I'm glad you like it. Let's eat, I'm hungry."

"Mind your manners. Say grace!"

Her husband bent his head and quickly blurted out a prayer he learned in childhood and still used.

"God is grace, God is good, thank you for this food, Amen."

Alice watched her man hungrily fill his mouth with food and begin to chew noisily.

He is annoying, but sometimes he just surprises me. I bet he bought this for my birthday. Still, he did it in advance. That must mean he cares. I wonder what he'll do now for a gift. I bet he finds some excuse to get away on Saturday. Well, I could have done worse. Too bad about us not having children. Was it God's will, or are we being punished?

"Alice, quit daydreaming and eat your food. It's getting cold."

Why the old fool! thought Alice. *Sometimes he just drives me crazy!*

* * *

The fall progressed, and Albert and Alice Green worked hard on their two thousand acres. They were fortunate to have plenty of water from the stream that ran through their ranch. Al harvested wheat and corn in the fields. He also had a few acres of oats. Along the river, he cut grass and stored it in the barn. Alice tended the garden and put up vegetables. She picked apples from trees that she and her husband had planted long ago down by the stream. Fenced off, on five hundred acres, was a small herd of steers.

There was sadness between the two of them; they both blamed themselves for being childless. They tried to hide their feelings about it, but when it did come up several times through the year, their arguments became more serious and embittered. They yearned to have children and to raise a whole houseful of them. To each one individually, it was a great failure, a huge emptiness in their life.

* * *

Another year passed, and spring came. Al noticed that his wife was going deeper inside herself. There were fewer smiles, fewer jokes, less bantering between the two of them. Al went to town and got a catalog at the general store. He went out back to a pretty little bench and table that belonged to the owners and sat down with sarsaparilla, a sandwich, and the catalog. Carefully he went through the women's section and picked out a hat, shoes, and readymade dress. This should cheer Alice up, he thought, an outfit just for her with no special occasion. Perhaps this would show how much he appreciated her.

Al waited a whole month, going into town every Saturday and asking secretly for the "package," which never seemed to come. When it did, things went badly. He drove up in the buckboard in front of the house. In his excitement, he didn't go to the barn to unharness the horse or put away the food supplies. Instead, he jumped off the wagon, gathered the packages, and ran inside the cabin.

"Alice!" called Al.

"No need to shout! I'm standing right here."

He went to the kitchen table, pushed some plates noisily to the side, and set down three boxes, which he stacked one on top of the other.

"What's that?" asked Alice suspiciously. "Did you

mail order for some foolish doo-dad again without asking me first? Did you buy some junky thing we don't need?"

"Alice, is that fair? I promised I wouldn't do that anymore. And I keep my promises."

"Yeah, until you forget 'em."

"Stop cooking, Alice, and come sit down and open your presents."

"Presents? What presents?"

"These, I bought them for you."

"It's not my birthday. Are you losing your mind?"

"No, it's not your birthday, it's not Christmas, but it's June, and the flowers are growing, the crops are coming up, the grass along the creek bottom will soon be high enough for haying. Can't a man buy his wife a present when he feels like it? What's our money for?"

"Not for foolishness, Al. I bet you went and bought stuff I don't want and don't need."

"Honey! Don't argue or insult me. Look at your gifts!"

Alice opened the first one with reluctance. It was a pair of new, brown, soft leather button-up shoes. She tried them on, and they fit.

"Al," said Alice. "The other shoes I have for church are just fine. I could have…"

"Dear, they look perfectly grand on you. Go ahead, open the next package."

Alice opened a round hat box and took out a colorful wide-brimmed hat covered with artificial flowers. She held it in her rough red hands and just looked at it.

"Go on!" exclaimed Al. "Try it on, try it on!"

Alice put it on her head; the hat covered her graying hair

that was bundled tightly in the back. The hat transformed her pretty, thin face and made her look totally different. Al told her so.

"What it makes me look like," said Alice, rising and going to a mirror hanging on a far wall, "is like a darn fool."

"It does not! All those other women at church will be plumb jealous."

"You expect me to wear this fancy to church? Show something off like this at my age?"

"I do," said Al. "That's what I bought it for. Now go on. Open the other package."

Alice looked in the mirror one more time with the hat on, scrunched up her face at her reflection, and took it off. She put it back in its box and closed the lid. Then she began working at the largest package. She took a kitchen knife and cut one end open. She unwrapped layers of white paper and discovered a readymade long-sleeved print dress with an embroidered bodice. Alice took it out, stood up, and held it for size against her slim frame.

"It should fit," said Al. "I went over and over that with Sam's wife at the general store. Mrs. Snyder guaranteed it. Try it on Alice. Go ahead, try it on. You'll be the loveliest lady at church this Sunday. Those women will be so jealous…"

At this point, Alice collapsed back in her kitchen chair and began to sob—great heaving, heavy sobs, of a person deeply hurt and disturbed. Al stood there looking at his wife, his smile of joy disappearing into a frown of worry.

"Alice! Whatever is the matter?"

She now sat bent over crying. A pin holding her bun in the back let go, and long hair fell down across her right shoulder. Alice raised her head and exposed a bright red face and painful eyes full of tears, which ran in ripples down her cheeks.

"How can I face all those women?" exploded Alice in a voice full of grief. "What right do I have to wear clothes like these when I haven't been a proper wife and born you a child? Don't you see, Al? They'll laugh at me!"

Despite the pain his wife was suffering, Al realized that she was still a very pretty woman at thirty-eight years of age, the loveliest of those who crowded the church on Sunday. When was the last time he told her that? Had he ever told her that? Perhaps he had taken her for granted for far too long.

"Alice! Don't talk so foolish! A pretty woman like you, the prettiest married lady in the county, has a right to wear anything she wants. And her husband, who saved his money, has the right to buy it for her. Now Alice, if you feel that strongly about having children, it's time we do it. The orphan train is coming to town next Saturday, and we are going!"

Alice looked at her husband. For once, she did not talk back. There was a long pause of silence. She still held the lovely print dress in her lap.

"Al," she said quietly, the tears and red face disappearing. "You really think I am the prettiest married lady in…"

"You're darned tootin I do and mighty proud of it too!"

"Al, you never told me that before."

"Well, it's time I started!"

* * *

Alice was wearing her new hat, shoes, and dress at the train depot. The platform was crowded with town and country folk waiting for the orphan train. Most were curious bystanders looking for some unusual entertainment on a Saturday afternoon. But the remainder were there looking for children to adopt. Many ranchers already had substantial families and were hoping to add to their workforce. Al and Alice Green were the only childless couple.

Any orphan children who found themselves in the Greens' home would be lucky ones indeed. They were the most successful farming and ranching couple in the county. Many had wondered for a long time why the Greens hadn't adopted, so foolish to wait this long.

"Have you come for a child, Alice?" asked Mrs. Snyder, wife of the mercantile owner.

She was standing upfront along with the Greens near the railroad tracks. Having come early, they were now being pushed and shoved from behind by the crowd. Mrs. Snyder turned around angrily. A strong-willed and opinionated woman, she had a firm sense of her place in the community. She held an umbrella and brandished the long object in the air with her right hand.

"Quit shoving!" Mrs. Snyder yelled. "You'll push us onto the track! Back up, I say! Back up!"

Those young people closest to Mrs. Snyder, now being poked with the tip of the umbrella, moved away.

"There!" said Mrs. Snyder smiling. "That's better."

* * *

By the time the orphan train arrived, it was late. Nearly half the crowd of bystanders gave up and went about their weekend activity in town. The Greens remained. Al noted that his wife was very nervous; her hazel eyes searched the track impatiently.

Perhaps this will be too much of a strain on her, thought Al. *What happens if we don't find the right children? Or if we find bad children? Like the ones Alice kept talking about, children who lied and stole and were incorrigible. Perhaps we should go.*

"Alice," said Al. "Maybe we should…"

"No! You got me here. We'll see it through to the end, no matter what happens."

"Alright, if you say so."

They heard the train and finally picked it out, far away down the track. They remained standing and watched its approach, following the line of smoke, marking the growing body of the train, listening to the forlorn sound of the whistle.

When the train stopped, tired-looking clergymen and their volunteers stepped down. They inquired and were informed the First Baptist Church would be their destination. Children began to come off the train. Boys came out of one car and lined up. They were coarsely dressed and of all ages and sizes. Alice studied them intently, but Al watched his wife's face. Next came the girls; many wore ill-fitting dresses. This time Al saw his wife's lips part as she made some remark he couldn't hear above the noise. Alice fell in behind the girls and stepped quickly along. The husband followed.

At the church, the boys lined up on one side and the girls on the other. A little boy ran toward the girls' side. A minister came forward to stop him. The child, no more than four or five, darted around the darkly clothed man with the white collar.

Al watched his wife closely, and he saw that she was paying attention to the little boy. And when the child reached what must have been his sisters, they hugged him and then protectively joined hands.

The largest and strongest boys were chosen first. Other children were not chosen at all.

"What happens to them?" asked Alice.

"They will be put back on the train," said Al. "They'll go on to another town to be chosen or not."

"What happens to those not taken?"

"I don't know. I suppose they'll be placed somewhere."

By the time the two girls with the little boy came forward, the crowd had nearly dissipated. Mrs. Snyder was still there.

"I want that little boy!" she said loudly enough for the ministers to hear.

"And his two sisters?" asked one of the frazzled clergymen.

"Don't want them!" said Mrs. Snyder. "I just want the boy."

"You can't split us up!" said the older of the two girls, still holding her brother's hand. "He won't go with you!"

"Well!" exclaimed Mrs. Snyder.

"We prefer not to split them up," said another of the ministers from New York.

The two girls, one nine or ten, and the other, about eight, were now standing protectively in front of their little brother, effectively hiding him.

"I am a respectable member of this community," said Mrs. Snyder. "My husband and I run the general store. We are well established. Do I get the little boy or not?"

"Ma'am, as you see, the three of them are much attached to each other."

"I can provide the most excellent home for that child!" exploded Mrs. Snyder. "Shouldn't your organization be more concerned with that?"

"Madame," replied an older grey-haired minister. "When placing out the children from New York, we try to keep families together."

"You can't take him!" cried the alarmed girls, still blocking their brother from view. "You just can't!"

"Now hush, children!" called the minister.

Al watched his wife step forward. She went over to the two girls and bent down. Kneeling, she spoke softly. But Al, and everyone else in the room, heard what she asked.

"What's your name?" asked Alice.

"My name is Mary," said the oldest, hesitantly.

Alice turned her head to the other girl.

"My name is Roseanne."

"And your brother's?" asked Alice in a very kind voice.

"His name is Tommy," said Mary. "And we aren't splitting up! Ever!"

"How would all three of you like to go home with me? My husband and I have a little ranch outside of town."

Tommy put up two hands and shoved aside the shoulders of his older sisters.

"Do you have chickens?" asked Tommy, thrusting his head and body forward.

"Yes, and a milk cow named Lilly, and pigs, and horses, and…"

"Would you let me see them?" blurted out the boy.

"Yes, and talk to them, and feed them if you want. And you can gather eggs in the morning, and…"

"Let's go with her!" said Tommy.

"Well!" blurted out Mrs. Snyder, who turned abruptly around and stomped out of the church, banging the tip of her large umbrella on the floor with each departing step.

* * *

The children had no extra clothing, only a few personal items stuffed in a cloth bag that Mary carried.

"When our parents died of the fever," said Mary, "they came to our flat and took everything. I managed to get some family pictures and this bag. Then they put us in the orphanage."

"I see," said Alice. "Right now, we can go and buy a few things. Let's think on what you'll need. We'll buy bolts of cloth for dresses, shirts, and pants. I sew fairly well."

"We can sew a little," said Roseanne. "Can't we, Mary? Mother was teaching us before…"

"We can't make dresses or shirts, but we can stitch some," interrupted Mary.

"Does he speak?" asked Tommy, pointing at the husband.

"Yes, young man," responded Al. "And you'll find I can whistle, play the harmonica, milk a cow, raise steers, plow a straight line, and sit astride a horse."

"Gee, Mister, that's a lot!" said Tommy. "Will you teach me to ride a horse?"

"If I see you're careful and you mind your manners, and do your fair share around the place. If Alice says it's alright, we might get you a pony someday to ride."

"A pony! Yes, Mister! We'll do what you ask. Won't we, Mary? Roseanne?"

"If they treat us well," said Mary.

"Awww shucks," said Tommy. "Anybody can see these are nice folks."

* * *

Al and Alice Green sat up front on the blanketed seat of the buckboard. The three youngsters sprawled in the back box. They bounced along the rutted dirt road back to the Green ranch. Alice was constantly turning her head and smiling broadly at the children. Al, who was watching his wife closely, relaxed as he saw the lines of happiness etched across her face.

"Well?" asked Al, getting his wife's attention.

She flashed her husband a grand smile. It lit up her face and made her even more radiant. Reaching a hand over, she patted him on the knee.

"I think it's going to work out just fine," said Alice.

BINSLEY SEWING SHOP

SPINSTER LADY

Elvira Binsley, with her long nose, thin lips, and strong chin, was probably the most ordinary-looking woman in the county. Even though she had flawless skin, perfect white teeth, and a shapely body, men couldn't seem to get past her plain looks to appreciate her other womanly charms.

Elvira lived in Denver, Colorado, in the back of her shop. On this particular April day, she was so sad and lonely that she could hardly draw another breath. At thirty-two years, she lived alone without any close friend or companion, and she was utterly and completely tired of it. Something had to change in her life because it was becoming too unbearable to endure. She must do something, think of some way, and devise some successful plan to gain a life companion, or die trying. And she must do it without revealing her ambition or telling anyone about it. For, if someone found out about her secret desires, she was sure people would talk, rumor would spread, and she would be made a laughing stock by every person in town.

Elvira made her living as a seamstress. BINSLEY MILLINERY AND DRESS SHOP was the street sign displayed over her place of business. Ever since she was a little girl and learned needlepoint from her mother, she had sewn and eventually excelled at it. Had it not been for sewing, when her parents died in a tragic mishap with a runaway buggy, she would not have fared so well.

Her father had run a livery stable, and her mother was a housewife. When they passed away, she made the decision to sell their house and livery. With the limited funds, she purchased the shop with the large store window and sleeping quarters in the back. Starting the new business meant to sew dresses and hats quickly and at competitive prices. At first, she struggled and nearly failed before finally succeeding.

Sewing and thinking of men, she asked herself if I can do well at business, surely I can find a husband.

It was during the completion of a dress, and the delicate process of hand-stitching, that she got the inspiration to add a new line of business to her shop. She realized that her talent could bring men to her. Certainly ranchers living in or near Denver would want to purchase and wear embroidered shirts.

Once the idea struck her, she immediately went to work. She was a real artist, and her talent inspired her. When the first three men's shirts were completed, she had a mannequin made of a man's torso and head. Then she took one half of her window display and removed women's apparel. She replaced that with the mannequin wearing a fancy floral design shirt. For decoration, she added a lasso, spurs, and as an afterthought, placed a Western hat on the mannequin's head.

The next step was to put an ad in the newspaper. As a natural progression of her sewing, she changed the name of her business to Binsley Sewing Shop. She didn't want to scare men away by mentioning women's dresses.

On the second day of advertising, she had her first customer.

"My ma gave me two dollars and said for me to buy a shirt," said a boy of about ten. "I like your shirts; could you make me one like that there in the window?"

"No need to use bad grammar, young man," said Elvira. "Let me take your measurements."

"Ma said not to come home without a shirt. I'm to wear it to church on Sunday and today's Friday."

"I'm well aware of what day it is, and I couldn't possibly finish…"

Elvira thought about it. Here was a male customer. Should she dare not complete her first order?

"The best I can do…ah…I didn't catch your name."

"It's Tommy Wallace, and you're the Spinster Lady."

"That's not a very polite thing to say," gasped Elvira.

The boy took a step back. Even he knew he had gone too far.

"Sorry, Ma'am," said Tommy. "But that's how everyone talks of you. I never heard no other name."

"You may call me Miss Binsley, Tommy. Now, how about if I promise to have your shirt done by tomorrow? Say, on Saturday afternoon at five o'clock. Would that satisfy your mother?"

"I don't think anything I do pleases Ma," said Tommy bluntly. "But if I tell her you're making a fancy shirt for me special, I bet she would like that just fine."

Elvira gathered the boy's measurements, and against her better judgment, put down a dress she was working on and laid out the material to begin the shirt. She decided on black with a fancy floral design on the yoke, curved arrows in red over the pockets, and red piping around the cuffs and collar. As she worked, she thought about what the boy had said. It hurt her feelings, yet she knew it was true; people had always shunted her off to the side. When there were church socials or Saturday night dances, she was the helper. She was the first to arrive, the last to leave, and always left to work alone or to her own devices. How she hated being called Spinster Lady. Tommy would be the first step in changing that unwanted name.

The boy came back the next day, accompanied by his mother. When she saw the shirt, she was delighted.

"Why, it's simply darling," said the mother. "It makes Tommy look all growed up and dignified. I just bet the other boys will be jealous."

It wasn't so much the boys but the other mothers in the church who were envious. Before long, there was a parade of boys of all ages coming through her door for shirts. This wasn't exactly what Elvira had in mind. And, she had to raise prices as two dollars was hardly making a profit, and the embroidery was time-consuming.

Along with the boys, eventually came the fathers. This was also a development prompted by the wives. At least her clients were becoming the right age. But unfortunately, they were married.

It was Saturday morning when she had her first eligible male customers.

“This here’s the place!” said one of three cowboys who shoved their way through her door.

The smell of stale sweat, horse, and whiskey invaded the air of Elvira’s shop. She rose to meet the men and noticed that not one of them was groomed for their visit to town. Shaggy hair hung down beneath Western hats, and unkempt beards in various stages of growth were displayed.

“Ma’am,” grinned the first cowboy exposing a gap with missing teeth. “We was wondering about buying one of your fancy shirts.”

“As you can see, gentlemen,” replied Elvira, attempting not to breathe too deeply. “I have a table over here of various styles. These are made in small, medium, and large.”

“I want that there shirt on the dead feller in the window,” said the first man.

“I want the hat,” said the second cowhand.

“I want them shiny spurs…ex-actly what I’s been lookin’ fur,” said the third cowboy.

“Gentleman,” responded Elvira. “I sell shirts, not hats and spurs. And the one in the window is all handmade and stitched and is an example of my very best work. I won’t say it’s not for sale, but it will be very expensive.”

“How much?’ asked the first man with the missing teeth.

Elvira took a deep breath and immediately regretted it. She let out a long sigh and closed her eyes.

"Twenty-five dollars!"

"What?" said the first cowboy. "I can buy a used saddle for that."

"Heck," said the second. "I can buy a hoss for that."

"Lady," said the third. "If he ain't gonna buy it, I will. Purtiest dang shirt I ever seen, all red, with that black trim and those pretty little flowers. I bet the ladies at the dance will…"

"I seen it first," said the man with the missing teeth.

The cowboy pulled out a wad of money and threw it down on the table in front of Elvira.

"I still want that hat," said the second ranch hand.

"And I want them spurs!"

"All right," said Elvira. "Ten dollars for the hat and five for the spurs."

It was twice what Elvira had paid.

The cowboys laid down the money and grabbed their possessions. Taking the shirt off the display in the window took some time.

"Looky," said the one buying the shirt. "That feller's all naked."

"Gentlemen," said Elvira, still not used to the odors emanating from the men. "Mind your manners!"

All three guffawed. She handed the cowboy his shirt.

"I recommend you men bathe before going to the dance. I don't think any female would…"

"What do you take us fur, lady?" asked the one holding his new hat in grimy hands.

"Say," said the man with the shirt. "Will we be seeing you at the dance? Maybe you'd let me escort you…"

"Out of the question," said Elvira. "But if I see the three of you cleaned up and sober…and…you still remember me…"

"Whoopee!" said the man holding the new spurs. "Lady, I won't forget. You bring your dancing shoes, and you just see if I don't ask you first!"

The men left the shop talking excitedly and all at once. All three spoke one over the other until their voices blended into one.

"Did you ever see a purtier shirt…just looky at my new hat…you ever see finer spurs…look at that hatband, bet she sewed it herself…if she can dance the way she sews, boys, we's in for a root-roaring time!"

Despite herself, Elvira was grinning from ear to ear. *Not exactly the kind of men or man I am looking for, but it's a start.*

* * *

It was after supper, late in the evening, and Elvira worked by lantern light, designing and putting together men's decorative shirts. She wanted to have a good supply of various sizes. The only way she could get it done, without interfering with her dressmaking and ladies' hats, was to work at night.

At the front door of the shop, she heard a loud thump. It was late, eleven o'clock. Her father had taught her to use the .36 revolver she kept loaded and hidden in the top sewing drawer. She picked it up and walked toward the front entrance. After all, this was the West, and a woman had a right to protect herself.

Looking out the large window, Elvira saw nothing at first and then movement. It looked like a little girl kneeling down. The seamstress jerked the door open, and a woman's prostrate form collapsed against it and fell into the threshold. The young girl looked up. Tears were on her cheeks.

"Please, lady, my mama's sick," said the child, "will you help her?"

Elvira turned and hid the pistol under cloth on her sewing table. Returning, the business owner went to her knees and bent over the sick woman. She looked to be in her thirties, dreadfully pale and thin; her dress was worn and dirty. Looking at the girl, Elvira could see the child was in a similar condition. The night was cool, and their thin coats were not enough to ward off the cold.

"Is your mother suffering from illness?" asked Elvira.

"Yes," said the girl. "I mean, she has been coughing, but…"

"Yes, child? Go on. You can speak freely."

"We, Mama and me got off the train two days ago. She, we, were looking for work. No one would hire us, and…"

"Where have you been sleeping?"

"In an old shack at the edge of town. But it was cold, and Mama brought me into town to find a place to get warm. But the men in the saloon were mean, and they…"

"Here, child," said Elvira. "Hold the door, and I'll pull your mother inside."

"My name's Cynthia," said the girl.

"Cynthia, don't worry. I'll help you."

The unconscious woman was dreadfully thin. It didn't

take great effort to pull her into the shop. Hurrying, Elvira ran to her living quarters and returned with a blanket and pillow. When the woman was covered and her head cradled, the seamstress turned her attention to the child.

"Here, sit in this chair," said Elvira. "I have some leftover chicken from a late supper. Give me a minute, and I'll be right back."

Returning with a tray, Elvira had a plate with drum sticks, a glass of milk, and a napkin.

"Here, child, sit up to the table and eat this."

Cynthia looked hesitantly at her mother, then licked her lips at the sight of the food. Sitting at the table, the girl picked up a chicken leg and devoured it hungrily. She took a drink of the milk and then hurriedly ate the second drumstick.

"Use the napkin, Cynthia," said Elvira. "It's all right. If you're still hungry, after I attend to your mother, I'll fix more food."

Elvira felt the forehead of the unconscious woman. She was burning up with fever. Applying a cold compress, the business owner realized this was beyond her control or abilities.

"Cynthia," said Elvira. "Up the street is Dr. Catterson's office. You go there and knock fiercely. When the doctor comes to the door, you tell him Elvira Binsley requests his immediate assistance and will not take no for an answer. Do you think you can do this?"

"Yes," replied Cynthia, "I think so."

"To make sure, repeat what I said."

Cynthia stumbled over the words.

"I'm sorry, child," said Elvira, "I'm asking too much. I'll write it down."

Jumping up, the seamstress found paper and pencil and wrote.

"Here, take this to Dr. Catterson. Hurry, Cynthia, your mother is very sick."

Minutes sped by, but no doctor and no child. Elvira knelt and held the wet, cool cloth to the unconscious woman's forehead. Then the woman's eyes opened.

"Sick, I'm so sick," said the prostrate mother. "Where's Cynthia?"

"I sent her for a doctor."

"Please, help me up."

"I think it best you lie here."

"You don't understand, I have no money."

"That's all right. Don't worry about that right now."

"Why would you…"

"Everyone needs help sometimes. Now don't worry…"

The sick woman, burning up with fever, passed out. Just then, the shop door opened, and in came Cynthia and Dr. Catterson.

"I can't examine her on the floor. You have a bed in the back room?" asked the doctor.

"Yes, of course," replied Elvira. "There is a spare room for guests."

"Good. I'll pick her up, and you show the way."

Elvira did as the doctor asked. Then she gathered several more lamps, lit them, and brought them to the guest room. Cynthia followed.

"The two of you, wait in the front," ordered the doctor.

They watched him open his black bag, then they left the sick room.

"Will my mother get better?" asked the child.

Elvira had the daughter sit at the sewing table. From the kitchen, she brought milk and cookies. Then she answered the child's question.

"Dr. Catterson has a very good reputation. If anyone can help your mother, he can."

Anticipating a bill, the seamstress went to her room and gathered cash money. After twenty minutes, the doctor came into the shop, wearing his coat and carrying his bag.

"Cynthia, is it?" asked the doctor to the child.

"Yes, sir."

"Suppose you go to your mother. There's a chair next to her bed. Will you watch over her while I collect my bill from Elvira?"

"Yes, sir, but…will my mother be all right?"

"She is very sick, child, but time will tell," replied Dr. Catterson. "Tell me, your mother is very weak. Has she been missing meals?"

"Father died in the mines," said Cynthia. "We lost our house, and I'm afraid…"

"I understand, child," said the doctor. "Now you go see after your mother."

When the doctor heard a back door close, he went up to Elvira.

"That woman has starved herself. I imagine she's been giving what food they had to her daughter. I've seen this many times. Exposure to the cold didn't help."

"What's wrong with her?" asked Elvira.

"She has lung fever. As weak as she is, it doesn't look good. Elvira, it was kind of you to let them in your rooms. Most people wouldn't. I'm afraid the hospital is full, and the city can't take one more patient."

"I'll care for them," said Elvira, and the response surprised even herself.

"That'll cost you," said the doctor. "In this case, I can't afford to work for free."

"I didn't expect you to, Dr. Catterson. What do I owe you?"

The physician told her, and Elvira paid.

"What about medicines?" asked the seamstress.

"I left two in the sick room. Instructions are on the bottles. Keep her warm, feed her hot broth, and give her warm water. All she can drink. I'll be back tomorrow and see where it goes from there. I hope you can afford this."

"I am alone in this world, doctor, as you and the town knows. A few dollars are put away for an emergency. I think this counts as one."

"What people have been saying about you," said the doctor, "doesn't seem to be true."

"And what is that?" demanded Elvira in a harsh tone."

"Do you really want to hear it?"

"Yes!"

"That the Spinster Lady is a miser and a shrew."

"Doctor, I didn't know I was the subject of conversation. But since you say I am, you can tell those people for me, to go to…to…Hades."

The doctor laughed and then walked to the door.

"Tomorrow, Elvira. And I don't care what they say,

either. For you to take in two strangers like this and pay the medical bills makes you a good woman in my book!"

So that's what this town thinks of me! fumed Elvira. *And after all those years volunteering at church and at the town socials. Well! From now on, there's going to be a change around here!*

* * *

Cynthia's mother, Elizabeth Bowman, did get better. It took several weeks in her sickbed, but with Dr. Catterson's expensive doctor visits and medicine, the patient improved. The first few days, it was touch and go, but the broth, solid food, and Elvira's constant solicitude saved the sick patient.

Lying in bed for weeks allowed patient and caretaker a chance to get to know each other. Slowly, the two women confided in each other. Over three weeks, a solid bond formed.

Elvira enrolled Cynthia in school, provided the child with new clothes, and prepared a daily lunch for her. Elizabeth began working in the sewing business, and the seamstress finally found a loyal friend she could trust.

A storage room was cleaned out for Cynthia, and the guest room became a bedroom for her mother. With Elizabeth's help, the output of dresses, hats, and men's shirts increased, and so did the business.

During the next two months, Cynthia, and later Elizabeth, attended church with Elvira. During that time, the seamstress declined to help with food or fundraisers. The priest, Father Rolly, along with women from the

Saturday night social, confronted Elvira and complained about her absence. She let them know she was aware of what people were saying about her. If they were going to malign her character, despite her years of volunteering, she would no longer participate.

* * *

It was a Monday afternoon. Cynthia, Lizzy, now going by her nickname, and Elvira were each sharing a task in the kitchen. Cynthia set the table while the two women prepared supper. They sat down to eat, and the conversation turned to their daily routines. Cynthia talked about her day in school, and Elizabeth shared the unusual visit by a bunch of rough cowboys looking to order shirts for the next Saturday evening social.

Afterward, Cynthia went to her room to study, and the two women returned to cutting and preparing fancy decorative men's shirts.

"Elvira," said Lizzy, "may I ask you a question?"

"Yes?"

"I don't want you to get upset with me."

Elvira laughed and then soberly stated, "It depends what it is."

"You told me so many times about your father and how you loved to dance. But since we came into your lives, you haven't gone. May I ask why?"

There was a very long silence. Elvira excused herself and then returned with a tray with cookies and two cups of coffee.

"That's a part of my life I have never told you," said

Elvia, sitting down once more.

"Are you going to tell me?"

"It's too personal."

"Elvira!"

"Maybe another time."

"Aren't we friends?" said Elizabeth. "Didn't I share the most personal parts of my life? I hate to see you holding back. I know something is bothering you."

"You do?"

"I do!"

"All right, but you must never…"

"Elvira!"

"Before you came, I was very lonely," confided the seamstress. "All I had was this business, and besides that, my volunteering at the church and the town dance. But…"

"Yes?"

"But I never seemed to make any friends. And…as I found out later, people were taking advantage of me. Worse, they were calling me a shrew and a Spinster Lady."

Despite herself, Elizabeth laughed. Elvira jumped up and, in anger, threw a cookie at her friend. It struck her in mid-chest. Lizzy caught it as it began to fall, then stood up.

"Elvira! I'm not making fun of you. I would never do that. I laughed because you're no shrew, and you may be single, but…"

"But what?"

"Darn it, Elvira. If you would go to that dance, put on some finery, I bet you would find a husband, just like that!" said Lizzy, snapping her fingers.

"I would?"

"I know it! All those years you have gone to the social, and all you ever did was stand behind that lemonade table. Don't you think it's time you danced?"

* * *

In thinking of a good man, Elvira thought of her father. At night, after supper, her mother would go to the piano and begin playing the latest songs. Elvira's father would take her hand, and they would dance. She realized that's why she always attended the town social. Missing her parents so very much, the music and dancing seemed to connect her to them.

Elvira thought long and hard about what her friend told her. Going to Lizzy, the morning after their heated conversation, she blurted out her decision.

"Lizzy, I'm tired of hiding and all those years standing behind that table serving lemonade; this time, I am going to dance."

To that end, both women worked on special dresses for the Saturday night social. When the next monthly dance came up, Cynthia, Lizzy, and Elvira walked to the schoolhouse.

For the first time that anyone could remember, Elvira did not volunteer or stand behind the refreshment table. Nor did she help with the food. Instead, she brought cookies, and after taking off a fancy wrap, she appeared in a flawless pale blue dress that showed off her figure. Lizzy and Cynthia were equally well dressed.

The other eligible ladies talked, and they noted something different about the Spinster Lady. For one thing, she was with friends. They had never seen her stand so straight and confident. She located herself by the dance floor as if expecting to be asked. Women snickered. Still, there was something different about her.

The band was playing—two violins, a guitar, a piano, and a banjo. Couples were swirling in a crowded circle around the open schoolroom floor. The three cowboys from the shop came through the door, and the one in the red shirt stood out among his fellows. Elvira saw them and remembered it was more than two months since she had waited on them. She noticed that they were greatly changed. Each had a haircut and a shave, and, as promised, the one who had purchased the spurs saw the sewing lady first. He gave out a loud whoop.

"Lady!" announced the cowboy. "I don't know where you've been, but I'm here sober and all dandied up and wearing my new shiny spurs. If'n youse willing, I'd be mighty pleased."

The cowboy extended his hand, and Elvira took it. Together the man and woman joined the dancers. This time the cowboy smelled sweetly of hair tonic. To the women crowded about the schoolhouse, this was an unprecedented shock. Not only was the Spinster Lady asked to dance, but she was actually waltzing gracefully. She made the awkward and sometimes stumbling movements of the cowboy nearly unnoticeable. Not only the women but men were eyeing Miss Binsley. When the music stopped, several more cowboys lined up, vying for the opportunity to dance. If there was one thing Westerners liked, it was a good partner.

The man in the red shirt was next, and he danced awkwardly and forcefully. Elvira made him slow down and gave advice. Within a few short minutes, the cowboy's dancing improved. Then the rough fellow attempted to hold the sewing lady closer. Elvira gently shoved with one hand at the younger man's massive chest and said something that caused the ranch hand to give more space. When the dance was over, she was immediately grabbed by the cowboy in the new black hat. This fellow could dance, and together they smoothly waltzed around the makeshift dance floor.

Couples admired the gracefulness. Men and women who were not dancing stopped conversation to watch the fellow with Miss Binsley. Something had changed about the seamstress, and people who had never paid attention before, stood, stared, and wondered.

"That's Miss Binsley," said Tommy proudly to his friends. "She made this here shirt!"

Lizzy and Cynthia, as newcomers to the town, had no trouble finding dance partners. Cynthia found that her schoolmates were there and in their Sunday finest. She paired off with friends to enjoy refreshments and the music.

For the rest of the evening, Elvira Binsley danced. Several times the seamstress had to say no and beg to step outside, get some fresh air, and sit down to rest her tired feet. Men brought Elvira and Lizzy lemonade. Such solicitation for Miss Binsley was disconcerting to some of the women, and many gossiped. Eligible girls wondered what had happened that suddenly they had such competition.

After eleven, Lizzy met up with her daughter and Elvira.

"I think it is time for us to go," said Lizzy. "Cynthia's friends are leaving, and I'm tired."

"Then I'll go home with you," said Elvira.

"Oh no, this is your night," replied Lizzy. "I want you to stay to the very end. You, that dress, and your dancing are quite a hit. I don't want you to ever forget this night."

"All right, then," said Elvira, and she smiled at her friend. "The dance won't last much longer. I'll be home then."

At about one, the musicians began to wind down. Elvira was exhausted, and she begged to sit through the last few dances. She had one rare moment when she was actually alone. And then a tall man wearing a corduroy jacket sat down beside her.

"Good evening," said the fellow, looking every bit a rancher. "I've been watching you. You dance very well."

Elvira looked up into the man's blue eyes. He was not handsome, but his deeply tanned face had character and strength. Despite her tiredness, her heart began to beat rapidly.

"I've been waiting and wanting to get a chance to ask you to dance, and now I see I'm too late."

The band leader had just announced the last waltz, and they had already played several stanzas.

"I am very tired," said Elvira. "But if you have really waited, I will dance with you."

The rancher put out his hand, and she took it and rose to her sore feet. She stepped gingerly to the dance floor.

"I've been admiring you," said the tall stranger.

Together they started across the floor. As a couple, they were exceedingly graceful. Those remaining, stopped to admire.

"You dance very well yourself," said Elvira.

"Thank you. I do love it. But my ranch is distant, and I don't come to town very often. I was going to the hotel when I saw you sitting there."

"My name is Elvira Binsley," she said.

Gathering courage, she looked up into the rancher's face. It was etched with deep wrinkles from years of working under the Western sun.

"I'm Sandy, Sandy Spencer."

"I'm glad to meet you," said Elvira. "For years, I have come to all the dances. I've never seen you before."

"Like I said, I own a spread twenty miles south of here. I don't get into town that often."

"I'm a seamstress," Elvira found herself saying. "I have a little shop…"

"I heard men talking about the fancy shirts you make. And may I ask about the dress you're wearing? Did you sew that?"

"Yes, I did, it's…"

"Very lovely on you," said Sandy. "Very."

The music came to an end, and Elvira forgot all about being tired and having painful feet.

"Well, I guess they're finished. Too bad," said Sandy.

Together they stepped off the floor with the last group

of dancers. Elvira led the way; she got her wrap from the coatroom and walked outside.

"Do you have an escort home?" asked Sandy. "I don't mean to be forward, but…"

"No, I don't," said Elvira. "It's just a few blocks away."

It was June. The stars were displaying their pulsing brilliance. A half-moon shone. The man and woman walked across the dusty street and onto the boardwalk.

"The few times I have been here, I never saw you," said Sandy. "You, I would have remembered.

"Usually, I volunteer and stay busy with refreshments. This is the first time I have actually…"

"Danced?" offered the rancher. "But why? You obviously enjoyed yourself."

Elvira laughed.

"I did have a good time. But I'll have to say "no" more often."

Sandy laughed. "Cowboys, with too much enthusiasm?"

"Yes," said Elvira. "And you, where did you learn to dance so well?"

"My sister. She insisted. Taught me growing up, and then she got married and moved away."

"How sad," said Elvira, remembering her parents. "Very far away?"

"To Colorado City. Her husband works in a stamping mill there for the mines."

"You must miss her."

"I do—since our parents died."

"The same with me. I mean, mine are gone too, and I miss them very much. It's been lonely…"

"I take it you're not married then," said Sandy.

"No, I'm not. In fact…"

She almost blurted out some indiscreet thing. What must he be thinking? wondered Elvira.

"I never married," said Sandy. "I'm astonished that someone so full of energy as you, and so attractive, is still single."

"I've been busy," answered Elvira cautiously. "After my parents' death, I had to work to earn a living, and I just haven't had time to…"

"I could see part of that," said the rancher. "But here in the West, there are fewer women; men are so insistent. I find it hard to believe that you…"

"I suppose it does sound foolish. But, I have had to work hard. All these years I've concentrated on my business."

"I see. It's also the same with me. Until now, I've had no time for courting. I'm thirty-six. Certainly, you are nowhere near that age. Perhaps, if you are interested…"

"Yes?" asked Elvira.

"Would you let me call on you?"

They came to her business, and the sign BINSLEY SEWING SHOP reflected sharply in the star and moonlight.

"When?" asked Elvira.

"Tomorrow is Sunday, perhaps after church? About two in the afternoon? I could rent a buggy and arrange a basket of food for a picnic. It would give us time to talk and get to know each other. After that, I must head back to my ranch."

"Sandy," said Elvira, "I would like that very much."

She didn't know it, but in the moonlight, the smile made her face light up. To the man standing before her, she looked very attractive indeed. He reached for her hand and held it tightly.

Elvira pulled away and looked up at the rancher in wonder.

"Please don't be angry," exclaimed the rancher. "My intentions are sincere. I'm far too lonely on that spread of mine."

"Even so, Sandy. I'm not a woman who allows anyone to take liberties."

"I know that, Elvira. You're a strong woman, and that is what attracts me."

With that, Sandy raised a hand to his hat in salute and walked up the street. He turned and called out.

"Don't forget, tomorrow at two!"

Elvira stepped back under the dark awning of her shop and watched the rancher walk away. She continued to observe him until he disappeared around a corner. Then with a new sense of hope for the future, she took out a key, unlocked her door, and disappeared inside.

Dear Reader,

If you enjoyed reading *Strong Women of the West (Anthology),* please help promote it by composing and posting a review on Amazon.com.

Charlie Steel may be contacted at cowboytales@juno.com or by writing to him at the following address:

Charlie Steel
c/o Condor Publishing, Inc.
PO Box 39
Lincoln, Michigan 48742

Warm greetings from Condor Publishing, Inc.
Gail Heath, publisher

Lightning Source UK Ltd.
Milton Keynes UK
UKHW012211110521
383564UK00001B/20